The Two Jungles

Delia Simpson

Cover Illustration: Keegan Blazey
Editor: Ana Joldes

ISBN-13: 9798532487222

Contents

The Daily Vale - Issue 1

An astronomer and a cowboy walk into a tavern. No, that's not a joke. It really is how this story started. Well, okay then, it *is* a joke, but you'll have to wait to hear the punchline. Interested? Read on...

Hi, I'm Vale.

1

Ever since I stepped aboard for the first time, I knew I was being ambitious. Even then, I was completely unprepared for what was to come. After just one night, there were more surprises than I could have imagined.

The ship I am sailing on is the *Leisurely Ländler*. We have a crew of six, including a cowboy and a marionette. But perhaps the most surprising thing to me was that the ship does not sail on the water. Ladies, gentlemen, and citizens otherwise, the *Leisurely Ländler* flies!

Rocket, our captain, is both brilliant and terrifying. She came out of an early retirement just to build the ship and is relishing every moment. She created it completely from scratch to Galileo's designs, or so he thought. None of his original paintings had jet engines on them.

Galileo's the one you have to thank for reading this. He's a genius and the one funding the trip. His goal is to chart every star and to draw up a map of the entire world! Who knows what other discoveries and scientific theories he will make along the way? I can't wait to find out!

I met Veroushka at the restaurant in the Astronomers' Guild. She's a mystery to all of us, but she's been through a lot. She didn't have any friends in the City due to her being different, but hopefully, that's something I can remedy. She needs our help. Hopefully all you readers can be as open-minded as I am.

Doc Holliday and Leira were late additions. So far, I'm not really sure why the cowboy and his daughter are here. He is a wildcard, and she seems distressed, but I fear that if I reveal my guesses as to their origins, I may accidentally reveal a dark truth, something they may not want. Perhaps this secret will finally be revealed in one of my later blog posts. Dear reader, you'll have to stick around to find out!

You can expect to read the names of the crew a lot over the next few issues, so don't worry about remembering them for now.

As for me, it's my job to inform, inspire, and amaze you with what we find, but don't expect me to alter the truth like *that other* paper. We're several days in now and have already been through a lot. The others are all recovering, which gives me time to write. So, I'll start with a recap:

The story begins on a warm, snowy day at the harbour. I was wandering the Beirasmus market...

The Tawney Parable

She'd been trying to get to sleep when they'd arrived.

Back in the town of Runaway, far off in the desert, Tawney wasn't used to the heat. It felt like weeks ago. Even for the brief period she'd lived in the City, getting to sleep had been a struggle. She'd never known why, but then, she had been a child. Now, a young adult, she knew exactly why it'd been so hard to get to sleep in the City.

As she rolled around on her uncomfortable stone ledge, jagged dark-green and black hair flailing around and getting caught in her mouth, the only thing she could think about was the next snarky line. *Don't care much for the room service. Who thought compulsory check-in was a good idea? I'll be having a word with the jailer about this.*

Her brain would go at a million miles an hour when it was trying to run away, trying to think of anything different, anything to distract her. After all, she was trying to get to sleep, and she'd been trying to get to sleep when they'd arrived.

Knowing that the same people who had broken into her small metal house and smashed her bedroom door down as she'd been sleeping, who'd dragged her over the hot sandy street, forced her into a carriage and locked her up in a dark, smelly dungeon, were on the other side of the stone door, was terrifying. The Blue Guard were supposed to protect people, yet the words 'protect' and 'people' seemed to be subjective to them.

Citizen folk often considered the runaways to be bandits, less than human. Even when she'd lived in the City, they'd always been warned of those who lived outside. They'd been told the patchwork walls were there to keep them safe. Having lived outside the City, she was sure the walls had a different purpose. *One woman's bandit is another woman's pundit.* She hated every last one of them. It was the rage at everyone who had lied to her that kept her awake more than anything else, but the sound of rifle shots and screaming, the clanking of the Blue Guard as they ravaged the town of Runaway, and the sight of her brother murdered in front of her burnt into her memory, certainly didn't help.

Living in Runaway had always been a risk. When you put a group of people who are all running away from someone in one place, sooner or later, they'll find you. *All dregs in one casket.* The

Sheriff of Runaway had kept them safe up until now. They'd even had a recent addition. The blue-haired girl was cute. The Sheriff had put her in charge of supplies. It was her job to scavenge the desert, looking for consumables. When she had more time, she'd sneak near the city walls and steal from the Blue Guard or rich people trying to go in and out of the City. If she failed, the town starved. Luckily, she'd been good at her job. Tawney had made a point to memorise everyone's favourites. The Sheriff liked roast desert boar, the Doc liked whisky-filled rum-buns, and the bartender liked ginger crush. She made a particular effort to stock those items. She'd never got round to asking the new girl.

But it was all gone now. Everyone in Runaway was dead. She was the only one left. *Hey, I could form a one-man bandit!* she thought. But the green colour permuting her hair meant that she was worth a lot to someone. She just had to sit tight until someone rich enough came along to buy her, and then just when they thought they had her safe… Tawney smirked at the thought of her plan.

And that's how the rest of her night went. Thoughts faded from raging anger to light witticism like a spectre flower, not knowing if it wants to open or close. Conversations and arguments, long since concluded, continued in her head. She ended each and every one of them with an insult so detrimental that it would surely have silenced her opponents had she used them at the time.

Old, broken dreams of living in the eternal forest resurfaced. Her wooden apartment in the wooden city had looked out towards the next wooden skyscraper. As a child, she'd imagined the lush flora on the far side of the desert with shining leaves and brilliant orange vines. Up in the branches—her tree-house. She'd have made it herself by scouring the riverside for driftwood and would invite over her friends, the local wildlife, for afternoon tea. Sure, she missed Runaway, but a home in the heart of nature was heaven. Those dreams had been squashed a long time ago.

The lantern in the corner flickered to life. She sat up and looked through crusty emerald eyes at the dull grey stone door that remained stubbornly shut. It had been that way for the last five weeks. In the rare cases she got spoken to, they did it through the bars.

A loud grunt echoed from outside her door. She took a moment to translate. Roughly, this particular grunt meant that it was time to get up and start work for the day. By now, Tawney spoke grunt fluently. The same grunt in a lower pitch meant that food was coming, and two grunts meant that she had three minutes to prepare for bed. *I wish my literacy tests in school had been in grunts.*

Tawney leaned forward and peered over the front of her ledge. A freshly rolled parchment had been placed in a small crate. She picked it up and unravelled it, revealing the string of letters, numbers, and characters that would form her job for the day. She blinked twice, trying to make sense of it, but it didn't help; they never made any sense.

She swayed and stumbled over to the small chair in the opposite corner, sat down, placed the parchment on the stand and stared down the array of wooden keys in front of her. It took a moment for her mind to kick in to locate the first character of the day: '5.'

Eventually, she settled into a rhythm, typing in characters one after the other: *Seven. Six. One. Six. E. Seven. Four. Six. Five. Six. Four.*

Already she was exhausted. She *needed* to be doing something else. On the next character, a '3,' she caught her finger in the gap between the keys. She reflexively pulled it back and brought it to her mouth. *Oh, fighting back, are you?* she mentally threatened the inanimate object. Going for the next letter, an 'A,' Tawney caught her finger once more.

Instinctively, she thumped it with her fist, rattling the whole table. She quickly glanced over her shoulder, but the Blue Guard outside didn't seem to have noticed. She closed her eyes to calm herself down before getting back to it.

Two. Zero. Four. Two. Six. C. Seven. Five. Six. Five. Two. E. Two. Zero. Five. Two. Six. Five.

To keep herself entertained, Tawney had tried to work out if there was any meaning to the letters and numbers she'd been pressing over the days. She'd given up after one time it was a recipe for tater-nut cake, the same she used to make back in Runaway, and a favourite of the undertakers. Someone on the other side of the door was having a joke or was really hungry. Now, she simply shut off her brain and typed.

Seven. Seven. Six. One. Seven. Two. Six. Four. Two. Zero. Three. Five.

Now Tawney had a vivid imagination, having once managed to convince herself she could communicate with manta-rats, but even she couldn't understand why she was performing such an innocuous task. There had to be some kind of meaning. The Blue Guard in the hallway had been particularly unhelpful and unsociable when she'd questioned them, emitting several noises that didn't require her being fluent in grunt to be translated.

Three. Zero. Three. Zero. Three. Zero. Three. Zero.

Instinctively, Tawney typed in a three and a zero a fifth time, cursing under her breath as the final two characters of the paragraph reflected light into her eyes, distinctly, not the ones she had typed out. Hopefully, no one noticed. The last time she'd got a character wrong had earned her a growling stomach for three days.

Four. Eight.

More hours passed. The prisoner breathed a sigh of relief, leaning in her chair and placing her tired hands behind the back of her head, scratching at the coloured strands that highlighted the tips.

She got up and stretched out her arms and legs, swinging them around in all directions carefully so as not to accidentally punch or kick the walls. After all, if a net traps an animal, it's hardly the net's fault. The clock had moved on a couple of minutes from when she'd last looked at it, so it was about time for…

Two more horrific gargled grunts emanated from outside her door. They hadn't given her the luxury of a toothbrush or a change of clothes to sleep in and rarely gave her the chance to clean, so as usual, she'd have to lay, sweating in her dirty grey jumpsuit. She walked over to the door and grabbed two of the bars with her hands, peering through at the stone corridor outside.

'So, how 'bout a night cap, eh?' she asked the Blue Guard. It wasn't the lack of interaction with intelligent life that depressed Tawney but the lack of quality in it. She'd probably have a far more stimulating conversation with a giant forest-cat. Subtly annoying the impenetrable guard was like trying to elicit a reaction from a patchwork metal wall by tickling it—fun at the time, but ultimately pointless and thoroughly embarrassing when you look back on it. That'd been a fun night.

The lower-pitched grunt indicated a negative response.

'Oh, come aawwwwnn,' she lamented in the same sarcastic tone as usual. This time, the guard denied her the satisfaction of a third grunt. She harrumphed and sauntered over to her bed.

Tawney awoke with a fright.

Nothing ever happened in the dungeons, especially at night, but this time, something was stirring in the darkness outside. She sensed it. It had made just enough noise to alert her subconscious. She listened carefully. *Focus.* Footsteps approached. She could just make out the clock—4:30am. Had she finally made one mistake too many? She prayed that they were going for one of the other prisoners, that they were just passing through, doing some sort of routine check, or anything that would mean she could go back to sleep. The door to her cell creaked open, and a figure, hidden by the darkness, pounded on it three times.

'Up!' it commanded. Tawney followed the order as fast as she could in her slightly delirious state, instantly regretting accepting sub-ordinance. As her eyes began to fully open, she analysed the man in front of her. He wore dreadlocks, a nice dark suit, and a rough smirk on his face.

'I know you, don't I?' asked Tawney. The man circled around her, ignoring her question. 'You're that fighter, right? I've read about you. What's the matter? Come to me for a real fight, have you?' she said, waving her fists in front of her face before lowering them again. 'Sorry, wouldn't hurt a luminon me.'

'Lucky Buster is the name you's looking for, missy,' he said loudly, so close to her face she could smell the toxic meyacot on his breath. Tawney was determined not to let his intimidation work.

'Where's the Šéf?'

'Big man upstairs has got a nice seller lined right up for you.'

'A new gaff! That'd make a nice change from my dungeon, wouldn't it? Will there be wine?' she retorted. He paused, thinking about what she'd said. Clearly, he needed some help. 'Wine… cellar? Oh, come aawwwwnn. This stuff's honey! Combination of being thumped in the head in the ring and toxic meyacot, I suppose. You should probably see a doctor about that. I'd recommend the one in Runaway, only you guys murdered him.'

His face remained a void.

'If only you weren't so valuable,' he commented calmly, hiding anger between gritted teeth, contorting his head sideways to face her. He grabbed her by the chin and stared deep into her dark emerald eyes. Tawney wasn't going to fall for it. She'd known men like him.

'Oh, you mean a buyer? Why didn't you say so?'

Smack!

The contact forced her to stare at the ground for what seemed like hours. She could feel an aching in her cheeks as slowly the stinging was superseded by sorrow. He may have the advantage right now, but in the end, she knew people like that would never survive. After all, there was no honour or skill in hunting prey that's already trapped.

'What I's heard is you's going to a nice big penthouse in the City,' he said whilst striding the length of the cell as if encouraging a crowd in the arena. The thought of going back to the City was haunting, taunting, and daunting—the ghostly wooden skyscrapers like sick imitations of the trees they used to be. It was a graveyard for those trees, infested with people who were desecrating their corpses. A dead jungle. That's why she'd never been able to get to sleep there. That's why she'd gone to Runaway in the first place. She'd meant to go further, to the eternal forest, but she'd never quite gotten there. That old Sheriff had been very persuasive.

'You can't hurt me. I'm too valuable...'

Slowly, she twisted her head back up to the sight of Lucky holding the door open for her. His two Blue-Guard cronies grabbed her arms, but she shoved them off, electing to take control of her movements herself. Like all colour-haired girls before her, she walked out of one prison and into another.

Final Hydration

All of Rocket's senses were overwhelmed with chaos, except for taste. But right now, and quite unusually, she wasn't thinking about her stomach. This time, she was only concerned with keeping control of her ship, the *Leisurely Ländler*, as it spiralled downwards through the storm clouds at breakneck speed.

The sound of the wooden hull being pounded by an onslaught of rain occupied her ears, accented by the occasional crash of thunder. Hard droplets of water bounced off the wheel and slapped her in the face like the invention she'd made to automate the process of putting her welding goggles on. Lightning tormented her visual cortex with blinding flashes.

The wooden deck by her side exploded into flames. She shielded her face with her arm, thankful that she'd been wearing her heavy-duty welding clothes. Normally, she'd have been thrilled with the fire. After all, she considered herself a connoisseur of combustion and a practitioner of pyrotechnics, but when lives were in danger that weren't her own, then it became concerning.

Rocket flipped over a lever, smashed a big rubber button with a mallet, and typed in some numbers on the typewriter, hoping she'd remembered to connect one of those controls up to something that might help the situation. Regrettably, she hadn't.

On the deck below, Vale, the journalist, was desperately trying to button up her camera case. At the other side, Doc Holliday frantically cranked a lever at the back of the ship with his right hand to build up more power manually to the jet engines, his left hand keeping his Stetson safe from the kleptomaniacal weather.

A bout of turbulence hit the *Ländler*, and it lurched lower. The intense movement threw Rocket over her wheel, dripping blonde hair stuck to her face. Shaking her head like a frantic puppy cleared her sight.

With one hand gripped tightly on a handle, she stretched over to the wooden edge of the ship, reaching for a length of rope. She swiped and missed, nearly slipping over in the process. She reached further and grabbed it successfully on her second attempt, passing it round the back of the wheel's pedestal and then around her body. She tied it up around her waist and leant back a few times to make sure her makeshift wheel-belt was keeping her securely fastened in.

The ship was still descending. The grey of the lower storm clouds fell above them, and the endless ocean fast approached beneath.

She screamed at Holliday to get the sails down, hoping her voice would be audible through the intense weather scherzo. She pointed at the sails quickly before returning her hands to the wheel. The cowboy took a cutlass from its stand and began climbing the rigging, the ropes flapping about in the wind around him.

A deafening crash of thunder echoed off the hull as a blinding flash of lightning struck the ropes.

Holliday swung himself to the left to avoid the flames it had created as a section of rope below him fizzled away. Rocket gritted her teeth as the rope snapped beneath him. The cowboy's body fell, landing with a painful thud on the wooden deck.

Vale ran over to make sure he was okay, grabbed the cutlass, and made an attempt herself. She was nimbler than Holliday, thanks to her smaller frame, and was at the top in just a few seconds. With a swift slash, Vale cut the rope holding up the sails and jumped down, the sail gracefully following a moment later and splashing the water on deck over her clothes.

With more control now available to her, Rocket pulled back as hard as she could, screaming. She leant back, forcing the wheel-belt to take her entire weight, but the shadow of the *Ländler* appeared in the dark water beneath them as they descended ever faster towards it…

The doors to above deck slammed open in front of Galileo, his brown frock coat becoming a shade darker, having absorbed several litres of water in an instant. He scanned his surroundings and the chaos that was the crashing *Leisurely Ländler*. The adventure he'd prepared so hard to put together seemed over already.

'*Mon Dieu!* Are you okay?!' shouted Veroushka, the marionette from behind him, a mixed look of concern and distress painted in white on her barked complexion.

'Do you need help?!' screamed Leira between the strands of her dark blue and black hair as it blew about in her face. Rocket yelled from the helm, ordering them back inside.

Crash!

The entire ship jolted on impact with the ocean. Galileo was thrown to the floor as the *Ländler* skidded along the waves. A chunk of wood cracked off the bow, sending splinters and smoke up in all directions. With every collision against a wave, the ship tilted more and more.

To his left, and to his horror, Leira was sliding down the diagonal deck towards the edge. Galileo scrambled along on his stomach after her and held out a hand. She rapidly scratched at the wooden boards, failing to find a grip as she fell over the side and out of sight. Galileo screamed out her name, terrified that she was lost forever. In a split second, he flattened himself to the deck and stretched out, leaning his hands over the edge. Leira grabbed on, her sudden weight threatening to drag him in along with her. Her eyes were fixated down at the ocean; perhaps she was preparing

16

herself for death or making sure her feet were still attached as they trailed in the water.

This was all my fault. I've caused the death of these innocent people, the people I'm supposed to protect. The thoughts raced through his head as fast as the waves below. He clung on harder.

'Hold on!' he instructed Leira, instantly regretting it. *Of course, she knows to hold on... idiot.* His thoughts returned to the guild and the taunting and bullying that had started it all.

I should never have planned this. They said I'd never be able to do it, and they were right. I'm worthless.

'Help!' he screamed over his shoulder, his grip slackening as the water barraged it, lubricating the gaps between his skin and hers. *I can't hold on! I can't hold on!*

Doc Holliday grabbed onto an engine lever and cranked it as fast as he could, raising the power to the jet engine on that side. Galileo felt the force build up beneath him, and with a sudden burst of flames, the *Leisurely Ländler* was horizontal again. Leira was flung on top of him. He lifted himself upright after the girl had rolled off.

Galileo ran up the stairs and over to Rocket, who was twisting and turning gear sticks on her control panel with one hand and still trying to maintain stability on the wheel with the other.

'Off the power!' he shouted to her. She shot him a look that told him not to tell her how to fly the ship.

'You should head that way,' came a calm voice from the side. Leira was pointing east. The storm in that direction was just as bad as where they were right now. 'Please?' she added politely.

They had nothing to lose. Galileo nodded to Rocket. With one foot balanced on a crate, she used both hands and all her strength to spin the wheel. Slowly, the *Ländler* turned east, and quickly, the storm subsided.

Galileo and his crew took a moment to breathe. He laughed nervously. As the rain stopped, droplets fell from his clothes. He lifted his arms to demonstrate to Rocket just how soaked he was. She laughed at him, but was, of course, just as soaked herself, if not more so.

He asked Leira how she knew which way to go as Holliday approached and placed a hand on his adopted daughter's shoulder. The girl placed her own hand on top of his to hold it there but shrugged at Galileo's question. She'd seen something in the water; he was sure of it. He asked her as much, but again she simply shrugged. How had the climate changed so quickly?

A chunk stretching halfway across the left of this ship was missing, there was smoke everywhere, and the scent of burning petrichor diffused through the air. The broken hull groaned against the calm waves.

'*Quel malheur!* How will we fly again?!' asked Veroushka. Galileo stared at the floor, knowing Rocket would have something to say. He felt pre-emptively embarrassed on her behalf. He could see her run off to the side of the control panel to excitedly extract her blow torch from its glass case.

'I'll fix it with this,' she informed the explorers with the kind of confidence that only comes with madness or stupidity. Galileo looked around. Each of his companion's expressions matched his own—confused and doubtful. 'Trust me. Come on, when have I ever let you down?'

They looked around at the surrounding disaster, which Rocket appeared to have forgotten about. She pointed her tool upwards and gave it a quick blast. A rope directly above her head promptly caught fire, causing an already precariously leaning mast to fall down and nearly kill her in the process. She ran back to where she'd grabbed the blow torch and grabbed her fire extinguisher from the glass case next to it, running back to extinguish the flames she'd 'accidentally' started.

It was late in the evening now, and the skies were clear. Vale had been hired by Galileo to document the trip and take photographs, but there was more to it than just another job. Life in the City had become so repetitive, and the last thing she wanted was for life on the *Ländler* to do that too. What Vale really craved was a new land. They'd been sailing through the sky for days now, and as beautiful as life above the clouds was, she was itching to get off the ship and explore.

As Vale made sure that her leather camera case had successfully protected the object inside, the rest of the crew tidied up the mess the storm had made. The rigging was now free of the sails she'd climbed earlier. At the very top was a crow's nest. She asked Holliday for his monocular and walked over to it, tugging on the rope to make sure it was still stable after the various fires it had endured. Confident that it was, she climbed up, surprising herself at how good at it she seemed to be. It was rare she found a skill she was good at, that being the main reason she'd gone into journalism and photography in the first place. But that was okay; she didn't have to be good at everything.

Vale raised the monocular to her eye and looked out portside, scanning astern, starboard and finally, ahead. *There!* Just on the horizon, the jagged green structures of a tropical island were becoming visible.

'Land ahoy, cap'n!' she yelled down to Rocket, instantly regretting letting go of her professionalism in front of her employers. Rocket didn't seem to notice. In fact, the inventor/captain seemed to relish Vale's temporary lapse into childish playfulness.

'Where away?' came Rocket's yelled response in a similarly ridiculous accent.

'Erm, just ahead.'

'Full sails!' the captain shouted, curling her hand up to her mouth and mimicking a musical instrument. Vale glared at her and then around the ship to remind her of their circumstance. The captain merely shrugged. 'Well, p'rhaps not me hearties.'

Vale rolled her eyes and began the climb down, mostly ignoring Rocket's moaning and rambling about not having some kind of horn.

She joined her fellow explorers and peered out into the distance as the parade of green trees lining the shore and the gleaming white beach in front of it materialised on the horizon. Noises of amazement escaped their mouths. Now would have been a perfect time to get out her camera, but... what even *was* a camera? There was only nature, and it was beautiful.

But wait, there was more to it. She spotted something right at the corner of the island. It looked like—

'The island's growing!' exclaimed Vale, pointing towards the very right-hand edge of the island. Galileo turned to her with a cynical look, describing in rather too much detail how objects in close proximity to one's eyes take up more of one's field of view. She refuted his ridiculous ramblings, insisting that the island was, in fact, increasing in size.

Finally, he saw it. Entire chunks of land were emerging from the water to the side and fusing themselves to the existing land. It was just like the revolving staircases Vale used to get to her home on the 37th floor of her apartment block, only there, the constant noise of the clockwork powering it was infuriating.

She turned to him, puzzled. Galileo had his mouth agape. He shrugged.

'All truths are easy to understand once they are discovered; the point is to discover them.'

She turned to Rocket, who suggested magic. Well, whatever it was, Vale was determined to find out all about this place and capture as many incredible photographs as possible. What sorts of weird and wonderful wildlife lived on this jungle island? Had anyone been there before, and why was it expanding right before her very eyes?

Flume at the Top

Doc Holliday switched off automatic punting as they approached the shore and took hold of the oars himself. He didn't trust Rocket's handy-work to be able to navigate the jagged knife-like rock formations emerging around them, despite the calm waves. Seated around the gondola, his companions eagerly anticipated their first new land. To his right, however, Galileo seemed on edge. Holliday had noticed the astronomer's aversion to green when they'd first departed, and now they were approaching an island almost entirely made up of the colour. Even though he didn't understand it, he didn't want his friend to suffer unnecessarily.

'Y'alright?' he asked in his calm cowboy twang. The astronomer twitched and nodded nervously, the movement of his head and the rest of his body contradicting each other.

'We're only staying here until Rocket fixes the ship, aren't we?' he asked, suggesting that one of them stay behind to help. Vale reminded him that he was the boss and conjectured that she would feel far safer on a mysterious tropical island that had appeared from nowhere than in the same place as Rocket whilst she was working. Galileo didn't seem convinced. Perhaps he needed a distraction?

'How comes the island's so tall?' Holliday asked, gesturing at a silver rocky outcrop at the top. He looked down at Galileo, his expression trying to become a smile. 'In haiku, if you please…' Galileo beamed up at him, *perfect*. He pressed his thumb to his chin, and then his eyes lit up.

'*Landmasses moving*
Pressing together, forced up
Millions of years.'

Galileo waved his hand passionately over the island as he recited his theory, almost as if he was conducting an orchestra, guiding it into existence through his powers of rhetoric.

'Er, "millions" is two syllables,' interjected Vale. 'Mill-ions.'

'No, it's not. Mill-i-ons. Three syllables.'

'I'm a journalist, a trained wordsmith. I write articles for a living. Trust me, it's two.'

'How could it be millions of years?' interrupted Leira, her question trailing off nervously. She'd been quiet for the entire trip. Everyone turned to look at her. She shuffled back slightly, perturbed by the attention, explaining in a stutter that to her, it looked like the land was rising out of the ocean and pressing onto the side in just a few seconds. Holliday smiled at her, unable to be anything but proud. Galileo was puzzled. She continued, asking what made the landmasses move and what forced them together in the first place, suggesting something in the water.

'*Plus lentement!*' exclaimed Veroushka, grabbing onto Holliday's arm. The small boat beached, and Holliday was thrown off balance. He toppled over the side and landed face-first into the sand. He groaned and felt his hands sink between the grains as he attempted to push himself back up again. Vale let out a hearty laugh from behind at his misfortune. This would take *days* to get out of his clothes.

After they'd anchored the boat, it took the team an hour to set up their four tents and get a small campfire going using broken sticks they'd found on the edge of the treeline. Leira and Veroushka had volunteered to share, maintaining the arrangement on the ship. Since the marionette didn't sleep, and there hadn't been enough room for Leira when she'd boarded, she had been kind enough to share her room and allow Leira to sleep in her bed.

By now, it was dark, but a soft blue glow from the natural meyacot fruit high in the trees bathed the beach in soothing cool light. The subtle splashing of the waves was accompanied by the benign buzzing of tropical beasts and the consoling crackling of a campfire. Galileo stared at the stars, and Holliday followed his gaze. They were brighter than he'd ever seen them, shining down like they were proud. *What would stars say if they could speak?*

The rest of his friends were deep in conversation, laughing as Vale told them a story about what she'd done the night she graduated from her photography course. As hilarious as Holliday imagined it was, he was too hungry and too tired to listen properly. He got up and brought his monocular to his eye, pointing it up towards the top of the island. A thin stream of water seemed to snake its way through the rock and disappear into the trees below. Finding it unlikely that he would find anything with medicinal qualities at that altitude, he decided that when they went exploring in the morning, he'd make sure to stick to the lower levels. The whole reason for his joining this adventure was to look for medical supplies to help Runaway, but even though he was now the doctor of a dead town, he could still gather supplies and create medicines for the crew of the *Ländler*. That, in and of itself, kept his mind occupied and gave him the purpose he'd been looking for since learning of the town's destruction.

He put down the monocular and returned it to his bandolier. Extracting a slingshot instead, he knelt in the sand and felt around for a stone to load it with and, with expert precision, shot down a meyacot fruit. He picked it up. The smooth blue flesh of its ovular body felt squishy in his hands. The citrusy scent rose to his nose and tickled the hairs of his nostrils. He trudged through the sand back towards his friends.

'Any y'all hungry?' he asked as he tore it up into five segments, some of the liquid inside dripping into the sand. He quickly handed out the pieces to prevent any more of its tasty juices from escaping or his hands getting too sticky.

'Bioluminescence! Delicious!' said Galileo as he tucked into the fruit.

Leira took and ate hers silently, with tiny, meticulous bites. The day she'd turned up in his surgery, she'd not even trusted a glass of water from him. Holliday didn't blame her at all; if anything, that was a good thing, but he was glad she trusted him enough now to accept the fruit.

Vale took hers gratefully, placing the entire piece in her mouth in one go. She always seemed to eat as if she'd never eaten before. As she chewed, she grabbed a quill from her pocket and scribbled down some notes.

'Always the journalist, huh?' he commented. She tried to reply but nearly choked in the attempt. Giving in, she gave him an awkward thumbs up. He moved on to Veroushka, but she shook her head with sad confusion as the strings attached to her hand pushed the fruit back towards him.

'*Je regrette*, I cannot eat, *monsieur*,' she said. 'Save it for later.'

Holliday apologised and complied, ducking into his tent and sealing the fruit in a soft-glass bag. He exited just in time to see Leira yawn, so he suggested that they put out the fire and all get a good night's sleep, ready for a busy day of exploration the next day. Everyone agreed and retired to their tents.

'Rarrghhhhhhhhhh,' came the weird groaning noise from outside. Holliday awoke with a fright and, within a second, had grabbed his revolver. Instinctively, he aimed it at the inner lining of his tent. The red cloth was no immediate threat.

'Rarrghhhhhhhhhh.'

This time the sound was accompanied by the rustling of his tent as if some storm were trying to blow it away. Holliday put two and two together—an animal. A large one. As slowly as he could, he zipped open the entrance and crawled out.

Four thick golden legs were connected to a scaly body, which in turn was connected to an impossibly long neck, towering over him. The creature's diamond-shaped head was bent downwards and nudged against the tent, using its nostrils to investigate. It hadn't noticed Holliday yet, so he took a moment to admire it, the first new species he'd seen up close since leaving the City. It occurred to him how boring the wildlife there was. Humans were just about the only free animals. All the other animals were pets or food, usually bought on the black market. Even the luminons that lit the streets at night were trapped in the light beams between the lampposts. Everything here was so *free*.

The reptile's skin was patterned almost like a jigsaw; yellow, orange and red, both scaly and furry at the same time. Holliday raised a hand and felt the ticklish texture of its skin on his fingertips. The giant reptile raised its head and stomped over to the line of trees. It scanned the canopy in what Holliday imagined was an attempt to look for food. It stopped as it detected something several branches back and proceeded to insert its head into the midst of the leaves.

The creature suddenly let out a heart-wrenching howl. *It was in pain!* It moved its two hind legs backwards and tried to remove its head from the branches, but it was stuck. The tree bent down with it as it pulled its head further and further away. Finally, the tree snapped back up, and the creature was released, trickles of black blood falling from its face where the sharp branches had scarred its face. It moaned again in frustration, sat down on the sand, and sulked like a hungry child. *Perhaps it was a hungry child?*

Holliday felt his eyes visibly widen with an idea. He ran inside his tent and grabbed the bag with Veroushka's portion of meyacot from last evening, presenting it to the creature in his hands as an offering. He smiled at it, forgetting that such an animal probably couldn't understand the complexities of facial expressions or the intricacies of body language. It raised its head to him and sniffed at the fruit before eagerly swallowing the thing whole in a worryingly similar manner to Vale. With his hands now free, he stroked the creature's face, analysing it up and down. To him, it represented everything good and beautiful—the ultimate freedom. It could do whatever it wanted to without the burden of a society or the fear of a predator. *Betty! That's what I'll call her!*

Almost as if to prove his point, Betty, now full and satisfied, walked over to the ocean and stomped around in it, water splashing off in all directions.

'Raaaarghh.'

All the muscles in her body relaxed, and she fell into the water, roaring with joy this time. *She's playing! Hehe, just like ole' Betty.* Holliday laughed to himself and placed his hands on his hips, finally getting a chance to look around the beach in daylight.

The blue glow of the bioluminescent fruit was no longer apparent in the intense sunlight, but the buzzing of the creatures within the jungle persisted, louder than ever. Heat warmed him from the sand below and the sun above, somehow in a manner less harsh than in the desert. The growing rocks seemed to have settled since last evening. The ocean was a perfect shining blue like the strands in Leira's hair, only slightly ruined by the broken half-wreck of the *Leisurely Ländler*. He sincerely hoped she'd take her time with the repairs. This was a sight, unlike anything Holliday had ever seen before. *What a place to live this would be.* He pictured himself living here with Leira. They could chop down trees to build a house together. He could teach her how to survive. For a moment, it was the best dream ever, but how long could that last? Where would that end? One day, he would die, and Leira would be alone again. He couldn't do that to her again. They had to keep travelling until they found somewhere more appropriate to settle. They could go as far as they liked, but they could never go back.

As quietly as he could, Holliday returned to the tents, unzipping each of them and quietly waking up his friends, excitedly urging them outside onto the beach. Within moments, he was joined by Veroushka, Leira, Galileo, and Vale, each with their mouths agape as they laid eyes on their morning visitor.

'Meet Betty!' said Holliday, gesturing towards the creature in the ocean. He could see the delight on their faces as they observed her playing in the waves.

'Betty?!' questioned Galileo. 'Why did you call it that?'

Holliday felt his face burn and turn red and was fairly sure it wasn't heatstroke quite so soon.

Vale ran back into her tent to get her camera as Betty turned around, her eyes meeting with the new people standing on the beach staring at her, but she was spooked. The creature removed herself from the ocean and stomped as fast as she could, vanishing through a gap in the trees.

Vale came out from her tent with her camera, a face of excitement turning to disappointment as she realised a wonderful photo opportunity had been missed.

'Perhaps we should head into the jungle, *mes amis*,' suggested Veroushka. 'We might find her again.'

So, with no time to lose, the explorers packed up their bags and ventured deep into the undiscovered.

In the Forest of the Blight

Tawney sat on the floor in the corner, backed up as tightly as she could to the glowing amber walls. The owner must have melted down pots of Honeywax and built their penthouse with it. She supposed it hadn't occurred to her new *custodian* that there were plenty of people both inside and out of the City that would have loved to make use of that money. The ceiling alone could probably have provided shelter for several less well-off families for many generations.

A woman in a cream suit and bow tie stood on the opposite side of the room by the door. The sound of her closing it momentarily broke the silence. She had a small but awkward grin on her face, like a child being forcibly introduced to a distant cousin.

She rubbed her hands together and tentatively asked if she wanted a drink. Tawney raised her head from her knees and glared at the woman. She was young, couldn't be older than Tawney or twenty. *How could someone like her get so lucky?*

'So, what's it you do then?' asked Tawney in as sharp and biting a voice as she could manage. The woman was clearly taken aback by the attitude and the accent. It turned out she was an actress, but her father was a businessman. She proudly explained that he had owned the most renowned building conglomerate in the City as if somehow it had been her own accomplishment that one-half of her parents had been successful. *Professional thief, got it.*

Tawney returned her head to rest on top of her knees. This person had clearly decided to buy a colour-haired person on a whim without really thinking it through and had no idea what to do with her. That's how the *people* business thrived, she supposed—taking advantage of the extremely rich, the extremely lonely, and the extremely stupid. By her books, the first thing equated to the latter two. If her sums were right, she almost felt sorry for her. *Almost.*

'Do you... want to do... anything?' asked the actress, rubbing her hands. This time, Tawney's glare was furious. She bunched her fists—oh, she wanted so badly to smash these wall down but quickly remembered her tried-and-tested tactic of snark.

'Yeah, burn down your house, then this building, then the City,' she replied before returning her head to rest on her knees. The actress laughed nervously before letting out a high-pitched, childish yelp. Tawney raised her head to see what was going on, more out of boredom than of genuine interest. Ash was looking down her own body and all over it, and then all of a sudden, an animal appeared. The manta-rat perched on the woman's shoulder, waggling the bony fins on its spine as it stared Tawney right in the eye from across the room.

The actress apologised for her small pet—named Robin—taking him and flicking him roughly into a tiny cage on top of a pinewood dresser in the corner.

'Scrawny little weasel,' she said. Tawney winced. The manta-rat paused for a moment before heading over to a spinning wheel and climbing aboard, obnoxiously penetrating the awkward silence with the constant hum of its mechanism. Tawney couldn't help but feel sorry for the pathetic thing trapped in its small cage. She could relate, but right now had to prioritise her freedom.

'What's *your* name?' asked Tawney, aiming her words right between her target's eyes.

'Ash,' replied the actress. Tawney rolled her eyes. Typical that the name should remind her of the burning of trees as if she didn't hate the woman enough already. 'Yours?'

She ignored the question.

'I'm sorry if they hurt you, but you'll have fun here. We'll have fun together.'

Tawney turned herself around to face the yellow walls. *Shut. Up!* She only wanted people to leave her alone. She closed her eyes and calmed herself down, asking if she could be left to get settled in.

Ash rubbed her face in consideration, nodded, and left the room. *Oh, to be so naive.* Once the door was fully closed, she resumed her thoughts, just in case she could somehow read them. She was grateful to be alone finally. Perhaps Ash wasn't all bad. *Was it really her fault?* Unable to decide who to blame for her current predicament, she instead decided to blame the entire City. She had to find a way out of it. She'd never felt more trapped by those walls. With every second she spent embedded inside this graveyard of flora, the feeling of needing a cleansing grew stronger and stronger. It was almost as if the people infesting the City were also infesting her veins and crawling around under her skin like parasites.

She stretched out her legs along the cold, marbled Honeywax floor and used her hands to crawl herself up the similarly marbled wall. She looked around; no windows. The natural aura from the melted honey lit the room amicably. The room appeared to be some kind of relaxation chamber: Nice chairs scattered around, a lush bovine fur rug. She dreaded to think how many trees and animals went into that, just so someone's feet were slightly more comfortable once in a while. Tawney skirted around the rug towards the door but had already pressed her hand against it by the time she realised that it too was made from a dead tree. She felt a shiver along her backbone as she slowly opened the door into the hallway.

The penthouse was a labyrinth, and Ash was the monster in the middle. As Tawney explored its Honeywax walls, trying not to get lost, she wondered just how much each and every dead creature she came across had cost. Black-market bounty hunters, no doubt. Ash even had decapitated heads of urban wood-bovine hanging in the corridors as decoration.

Finally, Tawney came across a door decorated with metal bars reminiscent of those in her cell. *Ironic Iron.* It looked more rigid than the others and had two locks at the top and the bottom. If any door was going to lead to freedom, it was this one.

Hearing footsteps behind her, she ran to it and frantically twisted the handle—locked. She searched the walls for a key—empty. She ran back to the door and pulled on it harder and with urgency. She pounded it with her fist, charged into it with her shoulder, but it didn't react. She took a deep breath, closed her eyes, and…

'What do you think you're doing?!' said the voice behind her as hands grabbed and twisted her around. Ash's face was a mixture of cross and deeply upset.

'What's it look like? I'm baking you tater-nuts,' retorted the Runaway fugitive. They stared at each other, Ash's lips trembling and eyes on the verge of tears.

Ash's eyes broke contact. She let go of Tawney's arm and stormed off for the relaxation room as fast as she could. For a moment, Tawney stood there confused before sighing and deciding that, with no immediate way out anyway, she had nothing better to do than to join her. If she couldn't get out by force, she'd have to convince this woman to help.

Ash was sitting in the corner of the room with her knees up and her head buried in them. The actress was crying silently. Tawney stood, not really knowing how to feel or what to do, but then, who would in this scenario? She winced at the irony of their positions having been flipped.

'Why do you want to leave? Why do all my friends want to leave?' cried Ash into her kneecaps, cracking voice muffled by pristine trousers.

Tawney skirted around the fur rug and sat down next to Ash, tentatively placing her hand on the actress's leg and resting a head on her shoulder.

Tawney apologised for the way this person had been brought up, being the victim of a privilege that she didn't know how to use, and everything that had happened to her that had made her resort to this, despite not a single one of those things being her fault. Ash turned to face her; all Tawney could see was a lost cause. Tawney wiped a tear from her cheek.

'I don't know you, I'm not your friend, and I don't belong with you. I can't stay here.' She got back up and made her way over to the door, pressing it open with the tips of her fingers. Midway through walking out, she turned back round to the girl on the floor, only to discover that she'd got up and was pointing a revolver at her. Tawney raised her hands instinctively.

'Really?' asked Tawney. 'You don't look too confident holding that thing.' The tears had temporarily stopped streaming down

Ash's face. She looked angry now, childishly angry. 'You'd only be doing us a favour now, Ash.' The aggressor slackened her grip as she considered Tawney's words, but dismissed them, gritted her teeth, and re-aimed.

Misinterpreting the action, Tawney sprung, swiftly grabbing the weapon with one hand and using the other to twist Ash around, forcing her to let go of it. Underestimating her own strength, Ash fell to the floor. Tawney aimed the gun at her.

'Bullets?'

'Three.' Ash replied, defeatedly staring at the fur carpet beneath her whilst explaining there were more in the drawer in a room down the hall. 'What are you waiting for? Shoot me.'

Tawney paused, taking a moment to realise what she was doing before lowering the weapon.

'Sorry, wouldn't hurt a luminon me.'

Tawney didn't spend too much time analysing Ash's bedroom, but it seemed much like the rest of the house. Oozing honey and covered in dead things. The thought of trying to sleep in here was spine-chilling. At least there was a window. She located the ammunition, and along with it, a holster. She quickly fastened it to her jumpsuit and stored away the bullets.

'Be careful with it. It was my mother's,' said Ash from the bedroom door. Tawney turned to look at the figure in the doorway.

'You're gonna tell them, ain't you?'

Ash dropped her head, not having to speak to relay her answer. 'Well, that's consumer loyalty for you, isn't it? Well, I better get

37

moving then, hadn't I?' she said, opening the window upwards, climbing out onto the small ledge and closing it again behind her.

At this altitude, the wind raged, and it was freezing cold. Tawney's thick green and black hair flittered around in front of her face. The trams and people below looked like ants crawling around in the roots of a tree; she hadn't realised just how high up she was. The building directly across was slightly lower than her current height in the penthouse. If she was lucky, she might be able to grab onto the roof and climb up. *Heh, if I was Lucky, I'd just get it over with and kill myself.* She scanned the mahogany skyscraper to see if there was a window below, but where there should have been a storey, there were only struts—whoever had the rights to the space between those two floors clearly hadn't built anything yet. If she could lower herself from this window slightly, she could spring across to that gap and then... well... she'd cross that bridge when she came to it.

Okay, Tawney... just pretend you're in the forests now. It wouldn't take long for Lucky and the Blue Guard to be on her trail, so, with no time to lose, she took a deep breath and jumped into the depths of the wooden jungle.

The Pool of Fears

A dense purplish-green monkey-ladder canopy of palm leaves crowned the jungle with an arched cathedral roof. The flowers were vibrant, and the sounds of the wildlife chirping a *symphonie fantastique.* Colours Veroushka didn't even know existed whizzed by her face like paint from a brush flicked onto the canvas. Sounds vibrated and bounced off deeply-ridged tree trunks and reverberated through her entire wooden body, pulsating with life; that was how the wooden girl heard. Fallen orange leaves crunched underfoot as they walked through this new world. She wondered if this was what being in *The Snickets* felt like.

But the trek through the lower jungle was equal parts arduous as it was beautiful. Every few minutes, Veroushka had to call out to Doc Holliday or Vale so they would help her over a particularly large log or to cut a path through sharp, jagged branches.

A breathless voice from behind asked Veroushka to go and stand beside a tree. Vale was grappling with her camera, which had managed to catch itself amidst some particularly prickly foliage. Once free, she mimicked adjusting focus and pressing the shutter button.

Veroushka yelped with glee. She'd enjoyed having her picture taken so much with the group before and now relished every opportunity she had to be in one. Vale had given her the first print of the group shot she'd taken when they'd lifted off, and Veroushka had spent hours staring at it every night since whilst Leira was sleeping in their cabin. Vale found a relatively flat area to set up on, and Veroushka rushed over to the trunk where her photographer had pointed.

She was too eager, however. Just as she was approaching, the string attached to her left foot failed to lift it high enough to clear a broken branch, and before she could do anything about it, she was face down into the mud! Within moments, Leira was by her side and helping her up. Veroushka wrapped her fingers around the girl's arm as she attempted to leave.

'Stay. Be in the picture with me, *mademoiselle.*' Leira looked at her for a moment but then wriggled herself out of the grip and went over to stand behind Vale. Despite the sudden and fleeting pang of sadness, Veroushka forced a smile back onto her face as Vale took the picture, quickly printed off the draft copy, and ran over to hand it to her. It didn't even matter that she was covered in mud. Any negative feelings she'd had from Leira's refusal to be part of the photo dissipated once Veroushka laid eyes on the picture. There she was, standing by a beautiful brown trunk several shades darker than herself and surrounded by lush trees. She stared at it, just as amazed and joyous as she had been the first time she'd seen a picture of herself. That feeling of seeing a moment in time captured in print forever never got old. Although only a snapshot of light, somehow, she felt it, smelled it and heard it too.

'I regret, I have nowhere to keep it!' said Veroushka, for a moment thinking that she may have to give up the picture, having only just laid hands on it. To her genuine surprise, not one, not two, but all three of her companions who were carrying bags offered to keep the picture safe for her until they got back to the *Leisurely Ländler*. Veroushka would have cried with happiness, except for the fact she had no tear ducts. She handed the photograph back to Vale, who carefully slid it into a side pocket of her camera case.

The team of explorers all reconvened to decide which direction they should head. With Holliday wanting to stay on lower ground to look for medical chemicals and Galileo wanting to get to higher ground to draw maps of the place and analyse their position, a unanimous decision was made to split into two groups. Veroushka chose to stay with Doc Holliday, not wishing to endure a difficult climb. Vale elected to go with Galileo, hoping to get some pictures of the view at the top, which just left Leira. Veroushka, of course, selfishly wanted Leira to go with her and Holliday.

'I must… go further up,' she said, so unconvincingly that it seemed like she'd surprised herself with the decision.

With a plan formed and agreeing to meet back at the beach by nightfall, Vale, Galileo, and Leira departed north towards the centre of the island, leaving Veroushka and Holliday by the tree.

'Looks like it's just me and you, partner,' said Holliday as he tipped the brim of his Stetson, gleaming at her and holding out a hand. She smiled back, the cowboy and the marionette wandering the jungle. There was something so wonderfully whimsical about that to her. Perhaps she could convince Vale to write a short story about it.

She took his hand, and off they went.

Leira, Vale, and Galileo fell into a pattern. Galileo led the way and would get caught in some thorns. Vale would put down her camera on the flattest piece of ground she could find and help him, and whilst this was happening, Leira would get distracted by the diverse variety of curiosities the island had to offer. She'd call Vale over, who would pick her camera back up and take pictures of them, be they flora, fauna, or a bizarre hybrid of the two. Galileo, in good spirits, would theorise as to their biology, how they came to take this form and how they might survive. Leira would listen intently at his musings.

'For what reason, I wonder, does this creature have five eyes?
For what reason, I wonder, is it twelve inches in size?'
Leira shrugged back at him.
'Notice the holes carved into the trees,

Formed perfectly so they can come and go as they please.

Or perhaps the animals adapted to suit it,

For who survives if not the most fit?'

Oh, how she would have loved him as one of her teachers.

'Very good! Not a falter, hesitation, nor a stutter. Now, do one in iambic pentameter!' quipped Vale with a smirk.

After an hour, Galileo had given Leira plenty to think about. That was good. She was afraid of not having things to think about. She'd only be left with bad things. Lots of bad things. She'd had a week in the town of Runaway, stuck in the middle of the desert after being betrayed and abandoned by her parents with nothing to think about except bad things. In some ways, being alone for a week had been the worst part of it. At least actually being kidnapped had only lasted an hour or so. At least then, she'd had something to focus on. Even the first few nights on the *Ländler* had been plagued with the memories of what had happened: The Blue Guard as they stormed the town, eviscerating everyone, murdering the Sheriff, chasing her through the desert. She daren't imagine what a soul might be driven to without something else to think about. With memories like that, what lengths would they go to to forget or to survive?

As they traversed higher, the trees became denser and the wildlife more curious. A green-haired mammal scuttled up a tree and jumped across to the next, right in front of Leira and only missing her by a fraction. Flying insects whizzed past her ears with such piercing loudness that she had to keep checking to make sure they hadn't actually flown inside.

After two hours of ascending, Leira was craving a rest but didn't want to seem like a burden by asking for one. How Galileo and Vale kept on going was a mystery to her. Perhaps none of them were confident enough to bite the bullet and be the burden, each begging internally that one of the others would ask for a rest first.

Miraculously and almost too conveniently, Leira spotted what looked like an archway of thorns out of the corner of her eye. Pink petals dotted brown branches, all pointing inside like a portal to a dream. She called out in front for her friends to wait for a second before heading over to it.

As she approached, a new sound cut through the usual wildlife —running water. She *had* to go towards it. Some natural instinct was telling her to. Ducking under the arch, she instantly felt warmer. Not in the temperature sense, in that she was about as sweltering as humanly possible, but somehow the atmosphere of the glade was comforting as if some great burden had been lifted. Although it was empty, it seemed full to the brim with life. She spotted the source of the running water—a stream flowed over the edge of a jagged rock wall far above her head and created a pool beneath, surrounded by a natural stone barrier. She walked over and sat on it, slowly leaning over to dip her fingers just below the surface, allowing the cool, clear liquid to cover their tips. A pleasant tingle cascaded through her.

She sank her hands and cupped them together, bringing them up quickly and splashing the refreshing water over her face. She used her reflection to locate stray dirt accumulated over the day and systematically cleaned it off. It was therapeutic, like washing away the old life. She watched as trauma, guilt, and worthlessness dripped simultaneously into the pool and got absorbed by its comparative vastness. She knew that wasn't how it actually worked, but it was comforting to view it that way.

'We must be near the top now. I think this is the big rock we saw from the beach,' said Vale, pointing up to the overhang where the water flowed over. Leira looked but quite honestly didn't fancy it. Why would she go to the top when she could stay here? It was so peaceful and serene, a scene, unlike anything she'd experienced. It felt like the thing she'd been looking for, or at least... part of the thing.

'Amazing!' exclaimed Galileo, staring at the water as it flowed between his hands and dripped back into the pool. It seemed to sparkle and glimmer as it fell. He theorised that it might be *vitazate*, the chemical of life.

'If this is where they source their nutrients,
It would explain the diverse state of life.
From where and how does stuff like this come from?
With growth like this, supplies are no doubt rife!'

Leira thought about it. Could this be why it had felt so good to her? Was it this vitazate chemical drawing her in? She thought back to the storm the day prior. She'd seen something in the water, something swimming. It was guiding her to this place, guiding them to safety, but she didn't know what it was. What Galileo said made sense, but Leira couldn't help but have the feeling that there was something more to it for her, something personal.

'We saw parts of the island forming as we arrived, could this chemical speed up the processes of life? The way you said animals change and landmasses move?'

Galileo stared at her, his eyes narrowing in a gaze. *Oh god, he thinks I'm an idiot. The teachers always said I should never have opened my—*

'Brilliant!' he interrupted. The next few sentences of his happened so quickly that Leira struggled to comprehend them. She got the gist, though: Human cells repair naturally over time, but vitazate was used in medicines to speed up the process of a variety of these cells, depending on how it had been refined. Bound to the chemicals in the drinking water here, and in such quantities, life, and perhaps even the island itself, was being created and evolving at an intensely magnified rate, and that's why the island had appeared to be growing. The water was literally the life force of the island: *Evolution Juice.*

'Except that would imply...' started Vale, cynically, '...that the island is alive? Is that possible? The water its blood and the trees its bones?'

'Well, that depends on your definition of alive. We must be accepting in our view of sentience. If the parameters for life change, we must change our understanding accordingly.'

Galileo slipped the rucksack off his back, opened it, and pulled out a small vial before collecting some from the pool for Doc Holliday to use later. He held the full container between the three of them and twisted it around so they could all get a look. Inside, the sparkling was even more prevalent. Leira asked if it was magic.

'Any sufficiently advanced magic is indistinguishable from science,' replied the scientist.

Leira looked at both Galileo and Vale through it and felt intensely curious, like she simply couldn't go without knowing more things. She was overwhelmed with a desire to ask questions, a feeling that was refreshingly… new. Where to start?

'Why do you look different through the water?' she asked. Galileo smiled a knowing smile.

'Good question!' he responded. No one had ever told her she'd asked a good question before. He turned up towards the sun, which shone through the trees and shielded his eyes from the strips of light that breached the branches. According to Galileo, light travelled at different speeds through different substances, and because it travels slightly slower in water, objects observed through it appear obscured or bent out of shape. *Amazing!*

'It's kind of like mortazine, the opposite of vitazate. It slows everything down. A rather unpleasant poison if you ask me, actually.'

'Is that what happens at night? Light is travelling slower? Is night just poisoned day?' she asked, simply unable to stop the waterfall of questions flowing. She heard Vale giggling off to the side. Galileo laughed nervously. *Oh no, that was bad. I'm stupid. I should never have been curious. He's going to tell me I'm wrong and that I should never ask anything again.* Leira began apologising instinctively, reciting lines she'd repeated a tonne of times before. 'You know best' and 'I won't ask stupid questions ever again' poured easily between her lips as naturally as Galileo spouted out poetry or Vale wrote articles. Surrounded by both of them, as well as Rocket and the Doc, she felt comparatively inferior in their presence. The astronomer cut her off.

'Getting things wrong is what science and discovery are all about. I get things wrong all the time,' said Galileo, explaining that he had once attempted to measure the exact speed of light by asking one of his colleagues to stand a mile away as they rapidly switched a lantern off and on. Everyone at his guild had laughed at him as he'd failed to get any meaningful results from the experiment. 'Measure what is measurable, and make measurable what is not so. I put it to you and to my guild that there is no being wrong, only not yet knowing. You would make a very good scientist! It is passion that is the genesis of genius.'

Leira worked out the words, analysing them one at a time. It sounded positive, but it couldn't be. Was there sarcasm? No. He couldn't genuinely mean his compliments, could he? She waited for him to say he was joking and that she was stupid after all. But it didn't happen. He simply smiled at her. If even he got things wrong, perhaps there was hope for her yet. *Any sufficiently advanced magic is indistinguishable from science*—is what he'd said? She hadn't understood it then; perhaps all he meant was that there was no harm in wondering without knowing. If science was wondering, then was discovery wandering?

Vale suggested that they get going, setting off back towards the archway they'd entered the glade from. Galileo concurred as he put his rucksack back on and started following, pointing out that it would be getting dark in the next few hours.

'And as we all know, that's when the light slows down!' Neither of them appreciated Vale's sense of humour.

The moment Leira exited out of the glade, the warmth deserted her, the temporary lapse into positivity along with it. They were replaced with a more familiar lack of motivation and feeling of inferiority. The same couldn't be said for the others. Excited at being near the top, Vale and Galileo ran on ahead. Leira simply didn't have the willpower anymore.

But then she heard a storm of screams and the crashing of rocks. When she looked ahead, Vale and Galileo were gone. Panicking, she ran over to where the screams had come from, only to find a drop of around 30 feet. Off to the side, a green sheet covered in fake grass swung from the branch of a tree—a trap, but luckily it had failed to catch them. Down at the bottom of the crevice, Vale was rubbing her bruises, and Galileo was holding onto his cut-up leg whilst desperately extracting out the contents of his bag for a med-kit.

Leira shouted down to make sure they were okay, Vale's reply indicating that they were fine, just bruised and cut slightly. Vale placed both hands flat against the vertical rocks they'd just fallen down.

'Listen, Leira. There's no way up here. We're gonna have to explore down this ravine to see if there's a route back to you.'

'What should I do?' Leira pondered.

'Just go back to the glade and wait for us there? Be careful. If there was a trap set... then—' she started. Galileo turned to her, realising what she was about to say. He gulped.

'Just… be careful.'

On Vale's instruction, she felt the corner of her mouth raise. Although clearly, she feared for her friend's safety, the thought of more time by the pool was enticing.

As Galileo and Vale set off down the ravine together, Leira walked back to the arch of thorns and headed inside, alone this time.

Trance Macabre

'R*egardez!* An orange flower!'

Veroushka beckoned Doc Holliday over with audible awe in her voice. The strings attached to her knees slackened as she knelt on a bed of fallen leaves. Holliday removed his backpack and laid himself down on the ground on the opposite side of the flower to Veroushka, both of them admiring its unique glowing properties. 'It is beautiful, is it not?'

'Yeah...' came a distracted reply from Holliday. He reached into his pack and pulled out a syringe with some kind of bubbling liquid inside, hovering it over the flower horizontally.

'What are you doing?!' asked Veroushka, reaching around to protect the flower from whatever Holliday might be about to do to it.

'Well, uh, it might have some healing or medicinal properties, ma'am. I was just gonna run some tests,' replied the doctor, gently trying to force Veroushka's wooden arm out of the way without snapping her strings.

'You will not hurt it?' she asked. He assured her he wouldn't before telling her that he was looking for the vitazate chemical. If the flower contained it, the compound would whistle.

'It won't kill the flower. I promise.'

Veroushka reluctantly retreated her arm. The liquid dripped out of the syringe, fell through the air and landed on one of the petals, which appropriately struggled under the weight as the solution glided over the faded white and orange pattern. The first two drops slid off the surface and fell into the dirt, but the third settled on top. They each leaned in closer, Holliday's face just inches from hers; she could see the warm glow of the flower on her nose. Both of them fell silent, listening for any sign of a whistle above the gentle rustling of the trees and the occasional chirping of exotic birds. Veroushka could feel Holliday's heartbeat resonate through the ground and coarse through her body, but the flower remained silent. Holliday got up and looked down at Veroushka, brushing the dirt off his leather jacket.

'See? No harm done,' he said, offering a hand to help her up, which she took gratefully. His expression became a frown. 'To be honest, I didn't know it wouldn't've killed the flower.'

'*Pardon?!*'

'I'm sorry, honey, but I gotta find that chemical somewhere,' said Holliday, an obvious regret in his tone. 'Without it, I may not be able to help any of the others if they get sick or injured.'

Veroushka was conflicted. She looked back down at the flower again. Why should something so beautiful need to suffer to help people? For all Holliday knew, it led as interesting, as rich and as complicated a life as he, or any of the *Ländler* residents, had. How much was that flower's life worth to him? Why prioritise their lives over this one? It was just not fair. She was experiencing a new feeling now—anger. Not at anyone in particular, just at the cruel injustice the poor defenceless creature was facing. It was only with luck that the thing was still alive now. Not knowing who to blame, she instead decided to blame herself. She shouldn't have believed him. She should have stopped him.

'You will not use that again on any living thing!' she demanded. '*Compris?*'

The cowboy looked down at her, with an expression she hoped, but highly doubted, was fear.

'*Compris*, ma'am,' he replied with a two-fingered salute.

'*Bon.*'

Wanted: Blue. Reward 500000H.

That was the message that had appeared on the screen embedded into the hunter's wrist armour two days prior. She'd almost dropped her oar into the ocean upon reading it. She'd rowed twice as hard to reach the island, eager to confirm that she wasn't imagining things when she got there.

Kalma couldn't decide if she loved or hated this new armour; heartbeat detection, hover-boots, and aim-assist were just some of the cool double-barrelled features it offered. But on the other hand, it was heavy and cumbersome; its bronze plating took hours to apply or remove from her person. It had been bought on the black market, access to which was just one of the many benefits of being a bounty hunter.

She'd rowed for days to get here. Hopefully, the treasure would be worth it. The island didn't appear on any of the forbidden maps in the City, so it must surely be rich. Why else would you hide an island?

Kalma twisted a dial on her bronze gauntlets until the indicator was next to her messages. She pressed a button, and slowly, the pixelated letters reappeared one at a time:

Wanted: Blue. Reward 500000H.

She'd been looking at it almost hourly to make sure she hadn't misread it. Opportunities like this one had started coming through every now and then and were always a good Honeywax-maker. They were broadcast everywhere and completed by whoever happened to get there first. Sometimes the people were high-profile criminals. Sometimes they weren't. All she had to do was capture them, take them back to the City, and hand them in to the Blue Guard. Colour-haired girls always fetched the best price, but this was insane, ten times higher than usual.

'Five hundred… *thousand...* Honeywax…'

A smirk appeared on her battle-scarred face imagining her rival —Surma. He and she had grown up together, gone to school together, trained together, and all of it was a competition. She'd won at *being taller* when she was a little boy. He'd won at *taking punches to the head before falling unconscious* when he was a teenage girl. Even transitioning genders had been a contest when they'd first discovered they were doing it at the same time, but eventually, they'd realised that wasn't a competition to win (but she'd definitely have won if it was). It was a friendly rivalry, but that made it all the more serious.

At the end of the day, none of it mattered. They'd always return to the tavern, drink pints and pints of toxic meyacot, and have a good laugh with their bounty hunter chums.

Finally, Kalma made it back to the clearing she'd made for herself. She exited the shade of the trees and emerged into the raw, unfiltered sunlight. She was already burning hot, her bronze suit totally soaked with sweat, so, to alleviate some of it, she removed her helmet and hung it from a low branch, finally allowing her scarred face to breathe some of the natural air.

Over her shoulder was a bag containing her exploits for the day so far. Most of the island's fauna were four-legged mammals and slow, not entirely unlike the bovine she was used to back home. They were an easy kill, however, and being at least somewhat exotic, their hides would likely fetch a fair price on the black market. She could probably convince some poor rich soul that they were worth more. At the end of the day, only the buyer has to be convinced of its value, even if the thing itself is worthless.

She'd spotted the true prize on day three: a big golden reptile with a diamond head and a furry scaled body, but it was fast. Whatever it was, it'd not only be worth something but would almost certainly earn her some jealous friends. She zipped open her tent and threw in the bag before placing her hands on her hips and taking a moment to breathe. She used the sunlight to gauge how much time she had left in the day, shielding her eyes as she did so. Probably just enough time for her to check her traps, re-set them for the night, and then one more attempt at tracking the creature before nightfall.

Her compound bow was leaning against a tree along with a sheath of arrows. She walked over to it and picked them up, counting each arrow to make sure she had all five. Together with her bow, and the vial of mortazine safely stored in the front compartment of her armour, they made an expensive and deadly combination.

She picked out one of the arrows and stared at the tip, carefully wiping away a droplet of blood left on the sharp metal by the last animal that had died to it; the arrows were so costly, she simply couldn't afford not to collect and re-use them. She gently pressed her thumb into it, grinning at the pain she was putting herself through to prove this particular arrow hadn't blunted.

There was a rustling in the trees above, and she snapped her head with perfect reflexes. She quickly nocked the arrow she was already holding and aimed up at the canopy, waiting for any life form to show itself. Whatever it was, it was dead meat. Even if it was just critters, it'd still be worth a few Honeywax, probably enough for a rummer or two, or at least it could be her food for the night. The hunter watched and traced the movement to the left, using only a fraction of her muscle to keep the bow primed. *Show yourself, you scrawny lil' weasel.* A flash of brown skin appeared between the leaves. She smirked.

Gotcha.

Kalma released the strings of her bow, and the moment the arrow was flying through the air, it had vanished in a puff of turquoise sparks. A fraction of a second later, the same turquoise sparks appeared amidst the trees, and with a satisfying screech, the creature was dead. Its body fell between the branches, managing to get caught on a particularly nasty-looking thorn. *Ha! Worthless creature. So useless it can't even die properly!* She kicked her heels together and jumped. Flames shot out of the soles of her bronze boots and incinerated the grass beneath her feet, but they propelled her up towards the trees.

She hovered in the air for a second, looking back to admire the scorch mark beneath her. She smirked and switched off the display on her gauntlet, the bounty message fading away. It was unlikely she'd come across the girl with blue hair on her ventures here; it wasn't the reason she'd travelled to this place, but she'd keep an eye out anyway, and if she did, it'd be a brag that would keep her belly full of rum-buns for years. After all, anything was possible this far from home, and that's just what she was counting on.

Holliday had assumed Veroushka would be hollow, and therefore, light. But as he struggled to lower her over the other side of a fallen tree, he realised she was anything but hollow. She had a strange concern for other species that was totally alien to him, even as a cowboy doctor. Then again, it reminded him of how protective he was of Leira. He didn't know how Veroushka was even possible, but it didn't really matter anymore. He didn't want to hurt her feelings. She was a complete mystery to him. He wondered if she could feel pain or if it was possible to dissect her. He'd probably need a chisel. How was it that she could only drink tea and eat cake in particular?

He let her lead him through the jungle, and whenever she got distracted by something, he quickly took his syringe out and tested any plants that happened to be nearby.

'*Docteur!*'

He wasn't lying per se when he said that it wouldn't harm the plants, but it was better safe than sorry.

'*Docteur!*'

He quickly turned his head in her direction, fearing that he'd been caught testing. In fact, she was staring down at a branch. Holliday emptied the syringe as quickly as he could and dropped it back into a pocket on his bandolier before making his way over to her. She was kneeling and had her light wooden arm up against the slightly darker bark of a fallen tree.

'Is the colour similar?' she asked. He considered and shook his head.

Apparently no longer interested, she began wandering off again, leaving Holliday struck with confusion and intrigue. He jogged forwards to catch up with her, having to duck beneath the vine she'd effortlessly walked beneath, and queried what she had been doing.

'Ah, you do not yet know why I am on this trip. One grows tired in the City, amongst the people,' she explained. 'I want only to find people like myself. I do not know where I come from. If I find a place with the same kind of material as that from which I am made, then I know I will have found my original home. My *lieu de fabrication.* My *make-place.* Alas, it is not here, so I must keep travelling. There is nothing for me in this place, other than the adventure, of course!'

They walked together for a while, and Holliday made an attempt to introduce Veroushka to the concept of biology, by which she appeared fascinated. He informed her of how sickness worked, how medicine worked, how life worked, and how death worked, as well as all the chemicals involved—vitazate and mortazine.

'These chemicals that you... synthesise... you get them from plants, yes?' she asked, stumbling over the difficult syllables.

'Err... some, yeah,' he said nervously, not wishing to disclose to her the sources of some of his medicines, of which many were living creatures.

'So, you could get them from fruits or leaves? The parts of plants that do not harm it when removed, yes?'

'Err... I guess so.'

'What about that?' she asked. Holliday walked a couple of steps further and squinted up, trying to focus on what she was pointing at with a barky-brown finger. Strange-looking vines clung to and twirled around a branch. He felt a tug on his bandolier. He instinctively turned and swatted it off, but Veroushka only wanted his monocular. He handed it over and helped lift it to her eye. She relayed what she saw through it to him. The vines were thin and wrapped tightly around the host, its emerald leaves shining in the sunlight. There were tiny circular flowers dotted around on it… no, not flowers, berries. They were red, and purple, and dark pink. Holliday took back his monocular and made his way over to the base. He looked up at it and planned a route.

'Do not hurt the vines!' yelled Veroushka from below as he climbed up. He felt around in his pockets for the syringe, hoping that she was too far away to see him use it on some of the berries. No sooner had they been coated in the liquid did a thin whistle pierce the jungle atmosphere. He ushered it to be quiet in case Veroushka could hear, using his sleeves to wipe away the remaining solution. He quickly picked off a selection of colours and safely stored them in an empty bag. He threw it down by Veroushka's feet before slowly making his way back to the ground himself.

Veroushka had picked up the bag and was investigating by the time he returned. She carefully manipulated her fingers, gripped the zip and slid it across, reaching inside with the same hand and picking up a single berry. Her face was angry.

'You killed them!' she shouted at him, holding the corpse of the fruit in front of his face.

'Err… no ma'am. Berries aren't alive…' he replied quickly, hoping his voice sounded convincing enough and that Galileo wouldn't correct him later. She seemed hesitant at first, but her face calmed slightly, her perfectly straight eyebrows transforming from diagonal to horizontal. She brought it to her nose and suggested that it might make a nice tea before returning it to the bag. She handed it back to him, and he took out one of the pink ones. Cautiously, he tapped it against his tongue. Nothing. Not a fragment of flavour or a tangible timbre. The whole thing went in, teeth clamped together, piercing the skin, the juices inside spraying around his mouth. It was nice, refreshing even.

But there was something else...

'Natural mortazine...' he said, the impact of the raw poison hitting him at the same time as the meaning of his own words. Back in the City or back in Runaway, anything that looked like food was edible, anything that was poisonous smelled of death, like a warning. The thought of it being dangerous hadn't even occurred to him.

The world spun. Trees bent around over his head and all around. The ground was above him when he fell down onto it. 'Stupid...'

Taste was the first sense to go. It felt like the deathly acid had burnt off the buds of his tongue. He had just enough strength left to lift himself up but was so dizzy he instantly fell forward towards a tree. He stretched out his arm to lean against it, but by the time he got there, the tree was gone. He clattered to the ground. Smell was the next sense to desert him, the distinctive musky scent of the jungle suddenly absent. Touch followed. The ground beneath him seemed to vanish. Veroushka screamed his name, but the sound cut out as his ears gave up too. In a blurry mess of colour, the missing tree slowly reformed in front of him, not with the rough texture it

61

had previously had, but smooth and abstract, like a drawing. He stared in horror as it grew eyes, a nose, and a mouth—a ghostly mutilation of a tree.

'Help me!' it screamed in a high-pitched child-like voice that was totally unsuited to its design, but then what had he expected a tree's voice to sound like? It repeated the words over and over again.

Holliday covered his ears with his hands and begged for it to stop. He turned, unable to look at it, only to find a yellow dragon-like animal towering over him. The first thing he thought, other than being the most scared he'd ever been, was that he recognised it. It was jagged, scaly, and covered head to toe in scratches, cuts, and arrow piercings. Deformed, but definitely the creature from the beach. Betty screamed 'Help me!' in such a deep voice that the discordant clash it produced with the tree's scream of the same words was utterly deafening.

What he found scariest about his own death wasn't the impending lack of existence. It was his ability to name each and every organ that was now shutting down inside him as well as the vital life functions they provided. At least he wasn't dying in ignorance.

The tree and the dragon vanished, but their voices remained a repeating echo in his dying brain. He was surrounded by nothing but that wall of sound coming from all around and yet nowhere. Was this heaven? Or hell? It didn't really matter. Either was fine for Holliday. As the sound faded and the last vestiges of existence ebbed away from him, he thought of Leira and the town of

Runaway. He'd let her down so many times already. What harm was once more going to do? At least this way, he wouldn't do it anymore, nor would he have to live with the guilt of not being there for his town when they needed him the most. Now, Leira was the only runaway left...

Woman vs. Wild

With the wind in her hair and an adrenaline-fuelled brain, Tawney scrambled onto the roof. She hadn't used most of her muscles in what felt like weeks trapped in her cell, and now the sudden use of all of them at once was a shock to the system. She looked down behind her. *Gods, this is higher than it was a second ago.* As far as she could tell, there weren't many other directions to go other than down and only two ways of going about that. She briefly considered the quick way, but the fleeting thought was dismissed before it'd even had a chance to fully manifest itself consciously.

She crouched down on the edge and looked out over the City, a gargoyle watching over a graveyard. How could a place be so full of life and yet so dead? The City was rife with so many wooden skyscrapers that even the smaller ones scratched the clouds like they were the corpses of trees trying to climb out of their graves.

Three buildings over, she spotted a service hatch on the roof, hopefully leading inside and to a way down. It wasn't far, but the jumps across were enough to be scary. She directed all the power to her right leg and propelled herself forward. The textures of the brown wooden roof disappeared, leaving hundreds of feet of dead air beneath her, heart skipping in time with her jump. Then, she landed, stumbled, and regained her balance on the other side.

She approached the next gap, working out how best to get across.

Jump. Fumble. Crash. Roll.

Unable to control herself, she fell flat with a thud, crashing into a mast and nearly bringing it down in the process.

Tawney used the mast to get herself upright and checked herself for injuries. Confident she was fine, she studied the object, running a hand over the grill on the front—its shining texture indicating it was a recent addition to the rooftop. She'd seen nothing like this before. The thing sprung to life, emitting a piercing shriek. It subsided, and then a crackling voice broke through—

'… fzzzzd… We know… crrrrz… return to… tssсczzzz… home… crrscvvv… after you.'

Her eyes darted over the rooftops with paranoia, but there was no one in sight... yet. She had to get to that service hatch. The lodgings would hide her from view, at least temporarily.

Using all her strength, she wrapped her fingers around the mast and tore it out with a scream of power, throwing it down in a storm of sparks. That felt good, satisfying the urge to finally be in control of something like she was taking on the world single-handed, and no one was going to stop her—and she'd win.

The third and final rooftop was significantly higher than it had looked from afar. She took a run up and leapt, gripping onto the edge, her fingers taking her entire body weight and legs dangling in nothingness. Imagining the drop beneath her made her feel sick.

She hauled herself up and dashed straight for the hatch, kicking off the lock and ripping it open. A tall blue figure snapped its head to look up at her from within. She jumped with fright. *Slam!* But now, the Blue Guard knew exactly where she was.

She ran, desperately looking for somewhere to hide. The door slammed open behind her. She jumped back down onto the previous roof and pressed herself against a chimney, hiding herself from view.

The gun by her side itched with temptation, but she needed to be quiet. There was every chance more Blue Guard were lurking inside. Tawney stretched out with her foot to drag the still sparking broken mast towards her and picked it up.

Steps thudded closer. Breath held tighter. The metallic ends of a foot appeared around the side. The guard's joints creaked and groaned as it carefully edged around.

Tawney reached up around its head with the mast, grabbed the other side and pulled down on its neck. The attempt at a headlock was feeble compared to the strength of the guard; the next thing she knew, she was upside down, the next—flying through the air, the next—a dull pain on her back as she crashed to the ground. She quickly rolled over and sprung back up again, the weapon still crackling at one end in her hand.

The guard paced towards her in jolted robotic motions. She swung left, right, left. With a lurch forward of the mast in a stabbing motion, she connected the sparks with the guard's blue armour. Its entire body became charged with static, stormy electric lines flashing over it wildly. The guard itself gyrated violently before it slumped to the ground.

Tawney froze. She wasn't sure this was exactly the outcome she'd intended. What did this mean? Was she now no better than the people she was running from? What were the rules in the fight for survival?

The mast now lay on the floor a useless stick, its electrical content having been discharged into her aggressor's body. Its metal chest was stone cold to the touch. She didn't know if they were supposed to have pulses or not, but she was sure it was dead.

The sound of two more guards emerging from the hatch led her to the conclusion that now was not the time for self-reflection. Morals could wait; survival could not. The hatch into the building next door was out of reach now, so she analysed the surroundings to find another way.

Focus. She engaged her reliably vivid instincts. The buildings became trees, and she balanced amidst the high-up leaves of a Jester's Oak. *There.* Three levels down and several skyscrapers over, a small balcony jutted out like a secondary trunk. It looked precarious, like it could collapse at any minute, but it was the only option. The shoddy workmanship was about to become her advantage. *Perhaps it was built by Ash's father?*

Gunshots fired off behind her and crashed into the walls causing splinters to fly. She covered her head with her hands instinctively and dashed for it, settling into a rhythm: jump—sprint—duck... jump—sprint—duck.

Finally, she'd made it to the correct building. All she needed to do was climb down to the balcony. She took cover behind another billowing chimney. The smoke was thick enough that they couldn't see her through it, but she couldn't see them either... or could she?

Focus.

Her instincts kicked in. The wind echoing between the buildings stopped and all her mental energy diverted to pinpointing the location of her targets. She took aim with the revolver at where she felt they were, the *sense* of their silhouettes glowing through the smoke.

Her two shots rang out, followed by the sound of metal clattering to the wooden rooftops. She peered around the chimney, staring at their corpses leaning precariously over the edge of the building.

Tawney emerged and wandered over, kneeling beside the dead guard. She peered over, the narrow balcony jutting out directly beneath her. She pushed one of the bodies over and watched as it fell further and further into the nothingness below. *Graveyard.*

She clambered over and let herself drop down onto the ledge, instantly shifting her body onto the wall to relieve all pressure from the surface she'd landed on as it cracked and crumbled away. She scuttled over, finally finding herself at the window. Its dark tinted glass gave away nothing as to what was inside; even her instincts couldn't penetrate it. She hooked her fingers under the frame, trying to force it open, but it wouldn't budge.

Only one thing for it. Eyes closed—fists clenched. Tawney raised her left elbow and smashed it, quickly turning away to protect herself from the flying shards as she fell inside.

When she woke up, the sky was spinning. Except, it wasn't the sky; it was the ceiling of a lodging that she didn't recognise. A crackling voice broke out from somewhere.

'... fzzzzd... Look out... crrrrz... any information... tsscczzzz... report... crrscvvv... green hair.' She was too delirious to register it. A man appeared over her, smiling. He looked neat and tidy, a stark contrast to the state of the face he was looking at if the stinging was anything to go by.

'D... do you mind not spinning, please...' she croaked between coughs. 'H... h...'

'Hello?' he asked, backing away towards the device from where the sound had come, pressing each and every button on the front.

'How 'bout a night cap? Just one glass... please.' She sat up quickly, suddenly remembering what was happening. 'Where am I?' she asked, shattered glass sprinkling over the floor as she stood

69

up. Tawney dashed for the door, but by the time she'd reached it, the man had sidestepped in front of it to block her path. He suggested that she stay here, where he could look after her and help clean her up, insisting that she was safe now.

Tawney wasn't convinced, but before she could answer, the same static sounded on the speaker grill. This time, it clicked in her mind. It was Lucky's voice, and the grill was the same as the one from the roof. How could that be here?

'What's that?' she demanded.

'Oh, it's new. Just arrived today!' he said proudly, picking up a letter and handing it to her. It was entitled 'Official Property of the Order of the City.' Tawney scanned her eyes over it.

Valued Citizen,

You now possess in your lodgings a new technology. Please set it up as per the instructions below. We will use it to keep you informed with all the latest important official information regarding the City, as well as the latest news headlines from 'City, The Curious.'

There was more, but she'd read enough.

'They can keep us up to date and tell us what to do. And it works both ways. How great is that! ' The man pressed a button on the speaker and began talking into it. 'Hello? Yes, the woman you are looking for is here if you would like to come and collect her.'

Tawney was appalled. He'd really just done that, given her away right in front of her. He turned back and smiled.

'Now, you wanted a drink? Toxic meyacot is banned now, I'm afraid, but I can offer you some bovine milk?'

She pushed the paper back into his chest, and he fell on top of the table. It collapsed with his weight bringing the speaker down on top of him and breaking apart on impact.

She ran for the door and slammed it behind her, exiting out into the stairwell and peering off down into the endless spiral. The number '27' was etched into the wooden wall. With a deep breath, she began her descent.

The staircase was endless, and she was getting dizzy. Her brain barely registered the numbers of the floors as she whizzed past them: 22—15—4—17. She caught a glimpse of her arms. Blood dripped from them, but she was adrenaline-possessed to the extent that she could barely feel the pain of her injuries if they were even her own.

16—12—10—25.

She sped up, pushing herself harder and harder and hardly able to feel her legs anymore. Her breath was on fire, begging her body to stop and rest, but she ignored it.

3—5—11—8.

Were the floors always jumbled like this? She could've sworn that was not how numbers were supposed to work. It made it impossible to tell how near the ground she was. Was she going mad?

An unmistakable reflective blue shone up from floor two, three more guards making their way up the stairs.

She skidded to a halt and dashed to the stair controls, flipping every lever. The stairs reversed direction, the three figures struggling to progress upwards against the grain of mechanical force beneath them. The one at the front tripped over, causing a domino effect whereby all three guards fell in an unscrupulous pile.

She switched direction, dashing towards the door to apartment three. She charged it down with her shoulder and a scream, tumbling over the dismembered plank as it fell in front of her.

The first thing Tawney noticed about the apartment was the smell. Not the sharp sweetness of Ash's place, but a more musky, earthy scent. She briefly looked around, knowing that if she thought too hard about the furniture, she'd not be able to stop herself from resting. It was darker and colder, the wooden walls the same as the exterior of the building, and the floor hard and rough beneath her feet. This building was just like a flower, with the prettiest petals at the top where everyone can see them, and all that's left at the bottom is dirt. Ironic then that the very few people who did live at the top, were in fact, the furthest away from the rest of society, conveniently hidden away where nobody could see them. She wondered if those pretty petals were penitent.

The resident of this lodging wasn't in, but the place was a mess. Tawney carefully guided her feet between children's toys and stacks of paper, cursing as the straw-covered floor scratched at her soles. Now over at the other side of the room, she mentally apologised to the absent owner before jumping and smashing through the window, out and back onto the rooftops.

Thankfully, at a lower altitude, the drop-off to the side was less terrifying, the wind less intense, and the sound less sparse. Trams sped through the streets, people swarmed the shops and restaurants, and that nasty smell of roasted urban wood-bovine wafted up from below. *Stupid senses.*

Tawney froze as something else rose over the rooftops. Like a mechanical insect, the black, floating vehicle crawled through the air, propelled by jet engines on three of its eight spokes. It couldn't have been more than 4ft high and 4ft wide, but somehow a Blue Guard was crammed inside. She looked in the other direction, only to find another of the things rising, rockets wheezing and droning as it tumbled and spun through the air.

Caught between the two *spider* drones, Gatling guns welded to the bottom of each, both aiming directly towards her, she instinctively ducked. Bullets flew above her head in both directions, and after a brief clanging of metal, the right drone exploded in a ball of flame. The other flew out of control and into a spinning frenzy, lowering quickly in altitude and crashing into a wall, blowing up on impact and taking a chunk out of the building with it.

'Do not...czzzz...leave...alive,' came the omnipotent speaker voice once again, but a brief glance around did not reveal the location of its originating mast. Lucky was everywhere.

More spider drones appeared out of nowhere. Tawney began running again. They chased after her across the rooftops, demonstrating a horrendous lack of control. She shielded her head as one skidded against the balcony of a third-floor restaurant creating a flurry of sparks and narrowly avoiding the patrons.

The spider drones swarmed around her. She needed to be at ground level where she could lose herself in the crowd.

Focus.

There! A thin pipe, running down the side of the next building across.

Now feeling like she'd done this a million times, Tawney skidded down a diagonal roof and propelled herself across the alleyway just as a spider drone flew beneath her. She landed on the other side and clung to the pipe with her hands, pinning her feet against the wall. She climbed down, taking large vertical strides.

Finally, she was on ground level. She'd kiss it if it were natural ground, but here in the City where it was made of concentrated sand, the idea was sickening. She'd expected chaos, a constant flux of people moving in every direction like it had been when she'd lived there years ago, but something was wrong. Instead, she was met with order. People queued up at market stalls and tram stops, not in random confusion, but in straight lines. *Too straight.* Children's school caps were placed neatly on their heads as they stood hauntingly still with their guardians, not running around screaming or playing with each other or even trying to steal rum-buns from the bakery stands like she used to do. If they didn't do that anymore, what *did* they do for fun? Nothing, it seemed.

She moved through the people, trying to blend in. It was difficult; she was sure she stood out, caked in injuries, but surprisingly, no one spoke to her. No one pointed, and no one laughed. No one even offered her help. This was *not* the City she knew. What had changed? What was new?

The Blue Guard hovered above and around her in their spider drones. *Gods, give it up already!* She kept on running through the crowds, shoving the people out of the way where necessary.

As the sun was going down, the luminons started to come out of their posts to form their light bridges. They didn't deserve that; they needed to be free. The next lamp she came across, she smashed with her elbow. The creatures inside dispersed up, causing the air to glitter around her.

On she ran, smashing up lampposts and freeing all the luminons she came across, not stopping to look back and not stopping to think about all the people left in the darkness behind her.

She ducked into a side alley and continued her smashing spree as a spider drone followed her in, metal limbs spinning rapidly and bouncing off the walls wildly. She shielded her head as another spray from the Gatling guns devastated the wicker bins, in which rested the belongings of some poor lodging-less person. She leapt over it as it rolled across the alley.

The alley narrowed, walls enclosing as she ran. It became tighter and tighter, and Tawney began to get the horrible feeling there may not be a way out at the other side.

Faster... faster... faster...

Suddenly, there was a vicious scraping and scratching from behind. For a moment, she didn't stop, but once she realised that the ominous sound of the spider drones following her had ceased, she dared a glance over her shoulder. The terrifying metallic vehicles were caught between the walls. With capsules too wide to continue the chase, the controllers inside spun in place like a manta-rat in a spinning wheel. *That one's for you, Robin, lil' buddy*. One day, she'd return for Ash's pet.

She looked down the alley from where she had just come, but there were no more drones in sight. She was trapped in the shadows, where no one from the City usually went. She'd been warned to stay away from *The Snickets* as a kid, but now she had no choice. She prayed to her forest gods that this nightmare might soon come to an end, that she wouldn't get lost, and that whatever was lying deep within would be kind. Forcing herself to place one foot in front of the other, she delved deeper into the darkness.

Murder, She Wrought

Any second now…

The hunter had been waiting up in the treetops for most of the last hour, and by now, the sun was starting to set. Patiently, Kalma balanced perfectly still between two branches, with her back pressed against the larger of the two trunks.

She had a calculated view of a well-trodden path, a path that she'd worked out the animals used to get to and from a river in a clearing. When they started coming through, she'd be ready, especially for that giant golden reptile she'd been hunting. It *had* to come through. That was the plan, and this was the time to execute it. For now, there was only silence, the gentle hum of the wildlife she had yet to harvest, and the creaking of bark as she adjusted her position. She considered whether it might have been better for her to have made her base up here amidst the trees. It would have been harder to pitch the tent, but at least she wouldn't have to fend off all manner of poisonous insects and vicious llama-bears, especially in the night-time.

The heat of the sun stung the scar on her face. She resisted the urge to scratch it, liking the dissatisfaction, a constant reminder of her own mortality.

A subtle clicking sound emanated from her gauntlets, so she gently twisted her arm to check it out. The flashing red dot indicated a heartbeat, not far away from her position. *Excellent.* Then, there was another, then another, then another, and before she knew it, a whole entourage of red dots was heading towards her.

A disturbance below. Kalma prepared herself, swiftly extracting an arrow from the quiver that clung to her shoulder and decorating the tip with her poisonous smokey-grey mortazine from a jar, perfectly preserved in the instant between liquid and gas. A moment later, her arrow was nocked and the bowstring pulled back as far as it would go.

At the first sign of movement, she released the arrow. A flock of deer-like animals came stampeding along. Her arrow blasted through the air and disappeared in a flash of turquoise electricity, reappearing in front of the first in the flock and piercing its skull, all within a fraction of a second. The animal squealed in pain. Blood sprayed. It collapsed, dead. Instinctively, the rest of the pack dispersed in every direction. The hunter cursed under her breath that it still was not the reptile. A stupid waste of mortazine.

With the slightest of movements, Kalma pressed down with her right foot, sliding down the branch to the ground. She stored her bow over her head and knelt next to the carcass to inspect it. Using a specially crafted hunting knife, she carved out a section of skin but got very little for her troubles.

She threw the knife towards a tree in frustration with a loud grunt. It embedded itself perfectly in its trunk. The scar on her face burnt with anger. The reptile was *hers*. She would hunt it down across the entire jungle and kill it, whatever it took.

She extracted a transparent vial from a compartment in her leg armour, smirking at the tiny insects as they buzzed about violently inside. *Time to break out the big guns.*

Holliday awoke.

He'd expected to be dead. The dark purple canopy confirmed he was still on the island, but that was just about the only pleasant thing present. The stream to his right was red with blood, the reeds surrounding it littered with the skinned carcasses of reptiles. Some were familiar to him, but mostly their scaly bodies had been mutilated and punctured entirely in the same manner as his earlier vision of Betty. Turning around, mammals littered the marshes in much the same manner, all dead, all gruesome. He screamed, but no sound happened.

Holliday awoke.

He was face down in dirt and leaves. It took a moment for him to realise that his senses and organs were all functioning properly, and this definitely was not another dream. He rolled himself over and breathed heavily, making a mental note not to eat weird berries ever again, even if they smelled like they might make nice tea. Veroushka stared down at him with as best a terrified and confused expression could be, painted onto a wooden face. He tried to process what had happened by repeating it to her, but it didn't help. Neither understood, but both managed to conclude that in their present form, the berries probably weren't much use either from a medical or tea perspective. But that wasn't to say that they couldn't be useful somehow. Perhaps Galileo would like to analyse them.

After taking a few minutes to recover, Veroushka and a slightly more wary Holliday continued their expedition through the jungle.

'This way, *s'il-vous-plait!*'

Perhaps the marionette's physical make-up made her immune to the human weakness of stamina, but even if that was the case, Doc Holliday found it embarrassing to be constantly falling behind the significantly smaller being. 'I've found something!'

'Yeah, I'm comin',' Holliday shouted ahead. He was still perturbed by the vision he'd had earlier. His mind was so focused on trying to solve it; he had barely any energy left for exploration. Nothing had ever affected him like this before.

It had been his job in the town of Runaway to look after everyone else, but who looked after the doctor when the doctor needed curing? The thought of Leira flashed through his head. She and her blue hair glowed a shining light in his memory, but he felt guilty about it. His own well-being was a lot of responsibility to place on a young girl. That wasn't fair. He felt selfish.

From where he was standing, it looked like Veroushka was on the edge of a tree line. He wondered if they'd been walking so much that they'd finally found the opposite coastline to the one they'd entered, but then he peered through.

Nope, nope, nope!

The scene from his nightmare stared back at him, only the stream that had once been blood red was now pure blue. The animals that had been skinned and harvested were now alive, peacefully munching contentedly on delicious reeds that gently swayed in the breeze. Llama-bears ran freely, playfully fighting with each other and singing their songs of delight. It was utterly terrifying. He edged back into the safety of the trees, but a tiny coarse hand clasped his pinkie finger.

'*Qu'est-ce qui ne va pas?*' asked Veroushka gently, smiling as she looked up at him. Holliday explained what was wrong to her, but she dismissed it instantly with the excuse that even if the exact place from his nightmare was right here, it was just that: a nightmare. It was nice that she was being confident for him. He followed her in warily, grasping onto her hand tightly.

As they trudged through the reeds by the stream, Holliday had the feeling they were being watched. Not just by the animals, who seemed to be assessing their threat level, but there was another presence. It seemed to come from below. *The island itself?*

He touched the revolver holstered by his side and wondered if the surrounding wildlife had any idea what it was or the devastation it was capable of. For a moment, he had the horrible thought that somehow the images burnt into his head might have been caused by him. A projection of the future? *What would cause me to do that?*

After a while, the wildlife returned to its consumption of the reeds, clearly having concluded that the cowboy and the marionette were of no threat. Holliday breathed out a long deep breath.

'Please. Ma'am. Veroushka. I need a rest,' he begged. Veroushka thought for a moment, and then her dark black eyes lit up.

'Clear a space in the reeds by the river for us to sit. I am too light to do it,' she said with a matriarchal authority that reminded him of Sheriff Eliza. 'Carefully!' This side of Veroushka was amusing.

Like a good cowboy, Holliday did as he was told, and before they knew it, they were sipping tea from Veroushka's flask, listening to the steady stream and the occasional satisfied moan of a feeding llama-bear. Its head ducked down into the water on its long, thick, hairy neck, waiting for marine life to take a wrong turn into its mouth. Taking inspiration, he searched his bag and found a pouch of beans, one of Rocket's concoctions; rip off the metal tab at the top, and the bag heats up the food... apparently. He shared a doubtful look with Veroushka before following the instructions he'd been given.

The explosion that followed shook all airborne life out of the nearby trees and terrified the nearby ground-dwellers, who promptly exited the scene in fear of their safety and survival. The tab flew sky high, Holliday squinting in the sunlight to keep track of it as it reached its apogee and fell back down to earth, landing with a clink just inches from his feet.

Much as he had been instructed, inside the pouch was now a fully cooked bean stew. A fresh billow of steam poured out of the opening at the top, and along with it, a semi-delicious half food, half-burnt sulphur smell, making Holliday's stomach both growl and churn at the same time. Trying not to think too hard about what he was putting in his mouth, he downed it in one go. It wasn't nice, but he still felt slightly better for it. *Thanks, Rocket.*

Veroushka giggled at him, which Holliday met with a puzzled look. He asked her what was so funny. After all, he was only eating.

'Another strange habit unique to flesh-beings!' she replied, indicating that he should give her the now empty pouch so that she could inspect it. As she nosed over it like a puppy, reading the instructions and ingredients on the side and investigating the remnants of its contents, Holliday explained the concept of sustenance to the best of his knowledge. By the end, she was almost in tears with laughter, except, of course, that she had no tear ducts. '*Sûrement pas!* This simply cannot be true! The more I learn about you, the happier I become that I do not share the same qualities! I cannot imagine having to eat for survival rather than enjoyment!'

Holliday rolled his eyes and began to relax as she continued drinking her tea. So far, he had not found what he was looking for. The journey was still early days after all, but as he looked at the marionette sitting opposite him rambling on about tea and cake, he was beginning to realise that maybe there were other things to find on this adventure than just medical supplies. Perhaps medicine was not the only way to heal a soul. For the first time, and just for a moment, he forgot about Runaway.

It felt like they'd been there for hours, but finally, Veroushka suggested that they pack up their picnic and start making moves back towards the beach camp. Rather reluctantly, Holliday agreed, not particularly looking forward to the prospect of carrying a heavy backpack back through the harsh wilderness but resigning himself to the idea that it was better to do it now than in the dark.

'All ready, *monsieur?*' asked Veroushka. He nodded.

'Rarrghhhhhhhhhh.'

The cry had a haunting tone rather than the pleasant, playful one he'd heard earlier. The two of them rapidly changed directions and ran towards the noise.

The moment he saw the body, all of the sadness came back. Runaway, Leira, Eliza, everyone he'd ever failed rose to the surface of his mind. And now Betty was dead too. Without even thinking, he approached her corpse and stroked, but then he noticed a gleaming turquoise. The arrow was lodged at the back of her diamond head, piercing the skull and poking out the other side. Her whole body was covered in fresh scratches and scars, just like in his vision. Up close, it looked like parts of her had been turned inside out, a truly gruesome sight.

Sadness mixed with anger and a hint of confusion cascaded through him. *Someone must have done this.* He removed his

Stetson and placed it over his heart, a single tear rolling down his face.

Veroushka approached and placed a hand on his shoulder, but he was too distracted to react. She was off on another rant, something about the meaning of the nightmare and a warning of some kind, but whatever it was she was saying, he didn't care.

'Just shut up, will ya!' he yelled. She looked shocked, startled, and terrified, but complied. 'I'm sorry, honey,' he added a moment later. 'I know you're upset too.'

Then he felt the familiar feeling of tugging on his arm. Veroushka, again.

'*Docteur*,' she whispered.

'What?'

'Shhh!' The tugging was annoying now.

'What?!' he repeated, turning to her. She looked him directly in the eyes.

'There's someone in the tree...'

Holliday's eyes twisted in their sockets up towards the branches. The bronze figure seemed too busy analysing their weapon to notice them.

'Hey!' Holliday shouted, at which the helmeted head of the figure snapped in their direction with snake-like reflexes. The figure jumped down from the tree and sprinted towards them. It barged into Holliday, hard shoulder pads throwing him through the air and into a tree. By the time he'd recovered, the figure had vanished.

'Perhaps now you will listen to me, *monsieur?*' said Veroushka with a clear passive-aggressive undertone. 'It is clear to me what your vision means. There is a killer here. We have just met them. The vision was a warning and a cry for help from the island itself. We *must* help it. We must find whoever that was and capture them to stop them from destroying all life here!'

'I'll take 'em down,' he muttered. The opportunity for revenge was enticing. He didn't have that for those who'd killed his friends and burnt his town, but he did have it for whoever had done this.

'*Non,* our opponent is strong,' replied Veroushka. 'We shall have to use cunning and intelligence. We must keep our wits about us as we traverse from now on. If it is a hunter we seek, then there are no doubt traps around every corner, are there not? *Allons-y!*'

And with that, she was off again, this time with purpose. He waited until she was out of earshot and took one last look at Betty before muttering under his breath...

'We'll see.'

The Scent of Music

The glade seemed even more beautiful now that she was alone, the colours more vibrant and the sounds more enunciated. Shadows of gently swaying leaves were cast down from the genesis of a burning pink sunset on the surface of the shining pool. They reflected back up at Leira, who stared at her own face. She was far enough away from the waterfall that the ripples were dispersing by the time they reached her. The wall of trees and bushes that formed the enclosure made Leira feel the safest she'd ever been.

Eager to feel the strange chemicals on her skin again, she cupped her hands together beneath the surface and brought them up to her face. The same refreshing wave flowed over her. *Science is magical*, she thought.

She shifted herself so that she was sitting on top of the rock wall and gently lowered her foot down the other side, cautiously dipping in the tip of her toe. The shock of cold could've woken a cursed princess. She trained her body to get used to it, lowering her foot a little further every second. Finally, she felt the rock beneath and concluded that it was just about deep enough to swim in. With one foot in and one foot out, she set her backpack against the dry side of the wall, removed as many of her clothes as she dared and set those on top of the wall.

She closed her eyes and pictured Betty playing in the ocean earlier that morning. Leira relaxed every muscle, finally letting herself fall over and into the water, mimicking the majestic animal.

The moment the soundscape changed was the most peaceful Leira had ever felt. She wondered why it happened, why suddenly all of the jungle sounds were now muted to her, and yet there was a constant humming and tinkling sound. She couldn't wait to ask Galileo. She felt her body float, just enjoying the sensation of letting the water carry her.

Her eyes opened. She had to open and close them a few times to get used to seeing underwater. The first thing she could see was the wall she'd fallen in off. She swam up to it, admiring every stone, every nook, and every crenulation. It occurred to her that her vision was somehow clearer underwater than it was above. She wondered what the reason for that was. The questions for Galileo stacked up; if only she had a quill and some parchment to write them down on.

She made a mental note to ask Rocket to make her some that worked underwater and preferably didn't explode.

She spun 180 degrees, pressed her feet against the wall and pushed, launching herself towards the waterfall. The currents hugged her skin as she flew, bubbles of air circling around her in formation. She curled her toes to cling to the bedrock and investigated them, watching as the bubbles rose to the surface in wavy lines, popping as they breached it.

A push upwards threw her above the surface, her water-soaked skin colliding with the intense heat of the descending sun, creating yet another new phenomenon: a pleasant tingle of cool warmth. After a moment, she fell backwards, quite deliberately back into the water, vaguely aware of the huge smile and massive enjoyment she was experiencing and thankful that no one was around to witness it.

She continued swimming for hours, but it felt like no time at all. Eventually, the sun fell below the tree line, and the glade became dark.

Leira sat on the rock wall, alone in her private glade. Silver strips of twilight shone down between the branches, illuminating the purple canopy and creating pink shadows across the ground as she wrung out her soaked clothes. She hoped, as she lay them out on top, that there was still enough heat in the air for them to dry. The delicate smell of rose delightfully diffused from steam as it rose from the glittering water. The jungle hummed with life like a krummhorn and the flowers that had grown into the stone behind the waterfall glowed in the moonlight. She giggled, realising that they must be *refracting* light. Refreshing refraction.

'Refreshing refraction, rising rosy rose, ripples rippling r... rosy nosey... r... r—'

Sigh. It didn't even matter she'd failed in her attempt to mimic Galileo. After all, getting things wrong was what science and discovery were all about.

She thought about her old life and how far she'd come in such a short space of time. Strangely, the thoughts weren't as painful as she'd expected them to be. The feeling of a positive present overshadowed the negative past, and what a wonderful feeling that was. Perhaps that was all it took, just some time. Time and magic water. She felt lucky having her pool of magic water here; it's not something that anyone else had.

All of a sudden, she had the urge for some music, so she reached down to her backpack and dug inside it, hunting around for her golden butterfly earpiece. It took a good thirty seconds for her to remember she'd given it to Rocket to mend. The thought of her captain made her smile. She'd love to have such chaotic energy like that.

She thought about the other people who made her smile: Galileo. Where Rocket was mad, brilliant and inventive, he was a blanket of calm, competent and wise. If she had his knowledge and her skill, she surely would be the greatest person who ever lived. That was the dream. It occurred to her that together they did make a wonderful pair, even if they didn't know it.

She was looking forward to resuming her hair braiding sessions with Veroushka. It felt good to play with her soft woollen strands. Although they'd not been travelling together long, the cold nights in their shared cabin where they'd sit together and play with each other's hair were the strongest memories so far. Her hugs were the warmest. She hoped the feelings were reciprocated but sincerely doubted it. *Who'd bother liking me?*

Still in the mood for music, there was only one thing for it. She looked around, making sure the coast was clear, pursed her lips and began whistling to herself. It was the tune of a song from her childhood that she'd first heard on her visits to the theatre and had fallen in love with instantly. But then she surprised herself by starting to sing the words.

'*Deep beneath the surface lies a different kind of life...*'

The lyrics cascaded into the air around her, her voice becoming more and more confident as she reached the second verse. As she sang, she began folding up her dry clothes and packing them away into her rucksack. She put on a spare set, which, luckily, Veroushka had insisted she borrowed from her. The long white and purple patterned dress she'd been given only fell to Leira's thighs, where it would have fallen to Veroushka's feet. Considering the temperature, perhaps that was for the best.

'*A world apart, but face to face. You and I survive together,*
An inch apart, but back to back. You and I will die together...'

Long echoing semibreves floated up between the trees, whilst the contrasting staccato quavers bounced from tree trunk to tree trunk.

A disturbance behind a nearby bush startled her; a chill down her spine accompanied it. At first, she thought it was just her imagination, so she continued to sing, but when two piercing eyes appeared between the violet leaves, she had to stop.

The two eyes and the long four-legged body attached to them leapt out, Leira only resisting the temptation to scream for the fact that it did not appear threatening. In fact, it was cute. The fur-draped deer seemed to stare at her in a manner that almost seemed disappointed. There was an awkward silence. The animal considered its actions before slowly making its way towards her. Should she move? Did it want to drink the water? She froze to her spot on the wall. It settled next to her, simply standing, but lowered its head and gently nudged her arm with it, stood back, and watched her. *Come on, Leira, don't be embarrassed by an animal.* Using the majority of her courage, she began singing again, although with more noticeable timidity this time due to the presence of an intelligent audience.

'*High above the silver sky, a watching creature flies...*'

The deer relaxed, shifting its body uncomfortably as it listened to her. Without even thinking, Leira patted her leg, and the creature came and nestled against it, taking a moment to find the right position before settling and closing its eyes. Leira relaxed, too, stroking its soft fur through her fingers and singing to it. It felt just like Veroushka's hair. Although she loved where she was right now, and the current company was better than average compared to what she was used to, she still wished it *was* Veroushka.

'*A world apart, but eye to eye. Hand in hand, we'll live out our lives...*'

Two small round orbs flew into the glade. The yellow birds landed on the rocks a few inches behind Leira, just out of sight. They placed their tater-nuts beside them and ate as they listened to her voice.

Now, tiny blue flashing circlets appeared around her head. Like fireflies to light, they seemed attracted to the sound, hovering around near enough so that they could hear, but not so near that they were distracting.

If Leira had been telepathic, she would have heard the two yellow birds communicating. She'd have heard them praising the talent of this unusual tall thin mammal, despite it being a stranger to these lands. If she'd had ultra-sensitive hearing, she'd have noticed the soft, low beeping emitted by the blue circlets, and had she been able to understand their language, would recognise their generally accepted signal of contentment.

In several hours, the birds would have told their bird-friends, and the circlets would have told their circlet companions. On and on the chain would go until even the fish would be humming her melody.

'*Through hardship, through misery and misfortune,*
We will survive...'

She addressed the final words of the song directly to the deer. The birds flew off back into the depths of the jungle, and the circlets blinked away.

Leira took a few moments to get her breath back. She couldn't help but laugh at herself. Never in a million years would she have imagined she would be capable of this, entertaining a beautiful animal on a tropical island, a hundred miles from home. Never in a billion years would she have dreamt she would want to be a scientist or a performer. A performing scientist! Last week's Leira would have scoffed.

Once she was alone again, she returned to the wall and packed away the last of her things. She laid down on top, listening to the sounds of the jungle continuing the song in the distance and watched as the last vestiges of sunlight seeped through the purple leaves before it set completely below the horizon. Now all she could do was wait for her friends to return and collect her.

Illegal Weapon

Holliday led.

Now that there was a threat, a danger, he felt the responsibility of going in front and protecting her. That was his duty, and perhaps subconsciously, protecting the marionette was a substitute for protecting Leira, and in turn, the entire town of Runaway. The more he thought about it, though, the more it didn't make sense. Veroushka was wooden, potentially even invincible for all he knew, and despite being physically fit, he was far more breakable than her. And yet, she was so fragile. Her perplexing biology continued to hurt his head. To solve this problem, he ignored it.

They made their way through the densest part of the jungle. With a machete in his right hand, Holliday slashed away at vines and branches, being careful not to hurt them too much for fear of activating the wrath of his short-tempered companion. With his other hand, he held his revolver. It was poised, ready with his finger on the trigger. If that hunter turned up again, he'd be prepared, Veroushka's feelings be damned. They walked in silence, accompanied by the ever-present chirping and buzzing of wildlife.

'*Arrêt!*'

Veroushka was frozen to the spot when he turned around, the strings as static as he'd ever seen them. She slowly raised her hand so that her palm was facing him. Confused but willing to play along, he took the signal and froze also.

The strings that controlled her knees slackened, and she was lowered towards the ground. The strings that controlled her hands slackened more and set them against the dirt. She closed her eyes, concentrating. He watched her, but she was completely still, focusing all her energy on the barely-trodden path.

'There is something nearby. I can hear the vibrations in the ground.'

'What?'

'I do not know. It is buried…' she said, indicating to her right. They followed her feelings, and sure enough, a few seconds later, Holliday, too, felt something. A regular pulse shook the ground slightly. It worked its way through his entire body and caused him to shiver. As he continued, it got more intense and faster until it felt like the source was right beneath him. He swiped away the pile of leaves and was met with a flashing green light, the object to which it was attached looking distinctly like…

'*Une bombe!*'

The green light flashed faster and faster, and so too did the bomb pulsate. On reflex, Holliday picked up the explosive and threw it as hard as he could, shouting at Veroushka to get down, advice which he promptly followed himself.

A silent explosion rocked the trees. Heat rushed over his back, but it was gone in a flash. The sound of trees rustling and birds fleeing faded as the explosion dissipated into the distance.

When it was safe, Holliday rolled over and looked up. The branches in the vicinity had been stripped of leaves, the bark now a burnt and charred black. Veroushka had failed to take cover, and her face was as scathed as the trees, but she appeared not to be too bothered. He supposed there was not much need for pain receptors on barked skin. She brushed her face, and the embers fell to the ground in a pile of ash.

'*Eh bien*, that was a close one!'

'You're tellin' me?'

'We shall have to be more careful, *monsieur.*'

'Whoever it is, they're playing with us, leaving traps.'

They carried on even more cautiously this time. Veroushka was right behind him, crashing into him several times when he stopped to aim his gun up into the branches at any sign of movement.

Hearing a rustling up ahead, this time it was Holliday's turn to stop her. He gesticulated with his free hand for her to stay put as he slowly moved forwards alone.

'What is—?'

'Shh!' he interjected sharply.

Spotting a bronze gleam in the corner of his eye, Holliday spun quickly on his foot.

In quick succession, he raised his gun arm in its direction and pulled the trigger. As he did so, a searing pain made its way all along his forearm muscles. He fell to the floor and dropped the gun. He clutched the wound, yelling out in agony, but knew better than to attempt a quick removal of the dart that was embedded there. His shot finished ringing out, echoing through the jungle. The body of the armour-clad hunter fell through the branches, flailing arms desperately trying to cling on to any of them but failing and clattering to the ground a few feet away.

Blood dripping down his arm, but willing the pain away, Holliday forced himself up and sprinted over to the figure who was trying to scramble themselves upright. He grabbed their hands and twisted them, forcing them to the ground and attempting to pin them down, but he was not prepared for their strength. With immense power from the hunter's legs, metal soles collided with his chest. Before he could have any further thoughts, he was lying on the ground, his entire body in shock. The faint image of a figure running off at lightning speed through the trees taunted his eyes.

But then it kicked in. He screamed in pain. It felt like his entire body was being slashed at, turning inside out. He'd never been infected before, but he recognised this feeling.

'Skin mites!'

Feeling the parasite begin to invade and attack his nervous system, he shouted to Veroushka, who rushed over. He guided her to the med-kit in his backpack, which she promptly opened.

'There's an auto-injector inside, just take it out and stab me with it,' he ordered as fast as he could, every word a struggle. 'Please! That will vaporise the creatures inside me!' The marionette obeyed but found manoeuvring her string-controlled hands in the confined space of the bag hard. 'Hurry! Ahh!' he winced, writhing around on the floor in an instinctive attempt to distract his body from his burning veins. Finally, she found it, hovering the syringe above the swelling wound on his arm, but hesitating.

'I don't want to hurt you,' she said with audible concern and panic.

'I'm dying! Again!' he thought he shouted, but with the remaining energy he had, it was more of a whimper. 'Do it! Now!'

She pressed down. He screamed, gyrating in every direction. Slowly, the fire coursing through him subsided, and the pain died away, leaving a pale, shivering ghost of a man lying on the ground, breathing heavily as he thanked the frozen stiff marionette.

He looked to his arm. She looked also. The dart that had contained the skin mites was still there, only now there were no creatures, just a bloody hole in his skin. In and of itself, it wasn't big, perhaps two inches in length and as thin as a needle, but it had lodged itself in on an awkward angle. He tentatively wrapped his other hand around the base of it and shared a look with Veroushka, pre-emptively wincing. He could tell she knew what he was going to do and thanked him for the warning by promptly turning to face the other way. He held his breath. *Boy, am I ever gonna regret this...*

Kalma turned around, making sure that the cowboy and his companion were firmly out of sight and sound, and then carried on even further just in case. Confident that she was far away enough, she found a rock to sit down on and removed her greaves. She'd felt the cowboy's bullet graze against her left leg, but luckily the damage seemed cosmetic. She was starting to appreciate this armour more and more, the more it saved her life. Observing that she was only bruised, the hunter replaced the armour and looked to her personal log device to analyse the data she'd collected from the strangers. She'd never used this function before, so she was keen to find out just how useful it was.

It told her that he was likely in his early 50s, probably intelligent, perhaps fast, and potentially a threat. *Thanks for being so conclusive.* Well, one thing was for sure, he was armed and was competition. The key word there being 'was.' By now, he was no doubt frothing at the mouth, the skin mites having almost certainly infested his entire bloodstream and turned him inside out. In a few minutes, he'd be as dead as that giant golden reptile. *Good.* Her mates back in the City were competition enough.

She pressed a button to switch over to her readings on the other character, but the screen was blank. Nothing. She hit it to make sure it wasn't a glitch, but it remained stubbornly devoid of information. No matter, she'd looked small, weak and feeble from the brief glance she'd had, whoever she was.

Kalma sighed. Her competition was eliminated, her targets had been exterminated, and her sacks back in the tent were stuffed with skins and hides, the rarity of which could keep her belly full with rum-buns and toxic meyacot for the next few months. And now she had the most valuable hide of them all. She practised her smug face for when she got back to the tavern to tell the other black-market bounty hunters of her winnings.

Now, there was only one thing left she needed to do before she could leave this island and return to the City, and that was to collect all her remaining traps. With no one left to run into them, it seemed like a waste not to retrieve them and use them on the next hunt, and besides, they weren't cheap. With that, she got up off her rock and began one last tour of the island.

It didn't last long. She returned to her camouflaged netting up by the glade, only to find it swinging from a branch, only no creatures were trapped inside it. *Odd.* She kicked her boots together and hovered down into the chasm below to inspect it, expecting to find some dead animal that had escaped her trap, but there was nothing there. *Focus.* She looked closer, examining the ground with an instinctive eye that only a hunter could have. *There.* A used med-kit lay hidden behind a fallen rock. She picked it up, inspecting it all over. This was not one of hers. Someone had clearly fallen down, which only meant there were yet more people here and only one direction they could have gone in.

Veroushka sat next to him on a fallen log. She softly sobbed in a tearless whimper. Holliday tried to ignore it, instead focusing on wrapping up his wound in a bandage, but he found it impossible not to wince with every sound she made.

He didn't have to ask to know why she was in this state. She'd wanted to capture this hunter to help the life on this island, and now Holliday had nearly died because of it... twice. He imagined she would be questioning her own choices, wandering what would have happened if he *had* been killed. The choice between him or the island. He knew she didn't want to make that choice, but she must have been realising that she might have had to.

At the same time, the hunter was still out there. Would she ask him to continue trying to stop them? Was the risk greater than the reward? The dreaded question, and the oldest moral puzzle in the world, whose life is more important?

He'd asked her to inject him, and she'd done so. But, he'd been infected with *living* creatures. Creatures, which she'd killed in the process. He knew she was averse to him harming any kind of life, but it had been them or him. She'd chosen him this time. He wondered if she'd worked that out. Would she make that same choice again? He wouldn't have hesitated if their roles had been reversed, no matter how painful it might have been or how many skin mites might have died in the process. That was his duty as a doctor.

The kindest thing he could think of was to give her time to work through it herself. He tied up the ends of his bandage and slowly set down his arm on the log.

As for himself, he wanted to capture the hunter even more. He'd had a reason before, but now, the skin mite dart to the arm had made it personal. He would understand, though, if all she wanted to do was return to the beach and wait for the others. In such a poor physical state now, he wouldn't be much use in a fight. He wouldn't be able to defeat them without her help.

With his non-injured hand, he reached into his bag and rummaged around for his clockwork pipe. He carefully lit it up and brought it to his mouth, but it was promptly smacked out of his grip by the marionette to his side.

'We need to get them,' she said, finally piping up. 'They have hurt you, and I will not allow it. Whilst they are free, none of us are safe. No life on this island is safe.' A decision, finally. 'We must find our enemy's base. Then, I have an idea.'

He smirked, nodded, and stood up, offering out his non-injured hand to help her up.

Climb of Duty

Galileo made his body as narrow as possible. He wondered how he'd managed to get himself stuck in this situation. Caught literally between a rock and a hard place, the latter of which also happened to be a rock. Then he remembered falling into a trap, down a crevice with Vale and not being able to climb back up again, leaving them with little other option than to follow it, hoping for a way up and around back to Leira. He held his breath and outstretched his hand to Vale, who promptly took it and yanked. Annoyingly, she was skinny enough to have got through without any help from him.

The rough textures of the rock-face scraped against the exposed portions of his skin. He cursed as Vale finally managed to pull him through, the force causing him to trip and fall beside her. He rubbed the scratch on his shin.

'Come on, it's not much further now!' she said, continuing ahead without waiting for him to get up again. He queried what she was basing her information on, but it turns out it was absolutely nothing at all. That seemed about right for a journalist.

However, after turning the corner, the grey of the surrounding rocks ceased. The *Ländler* looked almost like a painting as it gently rocked back and forth in the distance, anchored at the point they'd arrived at the island. It appeared exactly how he'd originally painted it in the designs. Well, apart from the smoke. Although, the more he looked at it, the more he could appreciate its present circumstance for having certain destructive industrialism qualities.

Beyond it, the ocean stretched on forever, a magnificent shining blue desert with fluid water-dunes. In front of it, a sheer drop fell away, down into a nebula of swirling violet treetops. Galileo got as close to the edge as he dared and peered over, accidentally kicking off a small stone in the process. He mentally thanked no one in particular that he wasn't following it. He backed off once he could bear the colour and the height no longer.

Over to the side, a narrow ledge decorated a near-vertical rock-face. About five inches wide and the exact opposite of smooth and stable, but it was the only way they could go. He found the word he was looking for: precarious. He looked over to Vale, who had also spotted it, but he didn't need to ask her opinion to know what she was thinking. With a roll of his eyes and a gulp of his throat, he bravely let her go first.

She pressed herself up tight against the igneous formations, angled her feet sideways, and shuffled along. Galileo held his breath, but Vale's nimbleness and climbing ability clearly weren't going to let her down. He didn't want her to fall, of course, but in the back of his mind, he wanted her to slip just a little bit... just enough so that she'd get scared and come back.

'What are you waiting for?' she asked with an infuriatingly smug smile. 'We can't go back; this is our only way of getting to Leira.' Her logic and reasoning were infallible. That seemed about right for a journalist.

With a sigh and hiding his nerves as best he could, Galileo approached the ledge and tried to mimic Vale's nimbleness. He pressed himself so tightly against the rocks he could almost feel them forming through him. He angled his feet so sideways it was unnatural and painful. Then, he closed his eyes, unable to cope with the sight of the height, and shuffled.

It felt like they were shuffling together for hours but could only have been about ten minutes, *the effect of extreme anxiety on the perception of time,* he theorised. The same reason being bullied back at the guild felt like it had lasted forever. He imagined that for the perpetrators, it had lasted barely any time at all. Still, he wasn't dead yet and was starting to gain confidence in his movements. Eventually, he was shuffling at almost the same speed as Vale, who remained remarkably undeterred by the ever-present danger.

He was concentrating so hard that he almost fell off when he bumped right into her. Startled, he regained his balance.

'Why have you stopped?' he asked as sharply as the drop right in front of him. She had turned herself around and was now facing the wall, analysing it up and down thoughtfully. Was she *trying* to give him a heart attack?! He prayed that she wasn't thinking what he thought she was thinking.

As it turned out, she was thinking exactly what he thought she was thinking. For all his ambition —setting out on this journey to prove to the guild that he could do it... well... perhaps they were right. Perhaps he couldn't. At the time, it'd seemed like a good idea; the discovery, the science, and the adventure of a lifetime. That was how it was supposed to be, but now, watching Vale prepare to ascend the cliff-face, expertly locating foot and finger-holds seemingly from nowhere, planning a route between them, he was starting to think maybe he wasn't cut out for this kind of life. She turned to him—

'Give us a leg up then.'

'How much further?!' Galileo shouted directly at the stone wall, lacking the energy to tilt his head upwards. It seemed like perhaps Vale scaled rocks as a daily occurrence. Perhaps it was part of her daily routine: wake up in the morning, brush her teeth, scale a cliff-face, take some photographs, and write a journal entry. He doubted she could hear him anyway; the wind was far too strong this high up. He adjusted his slipping grip, clutching at the hand-hold with the tips of his fingers to bring himself even further in to the wall.

'I'm nearly there, get a move on!' came the taunting voice from several metres above, the wind carrying it down. Carefully, he angled his head upwards to find another divot to grab onto. Having found one, he reached up and then tilted his head down to do the same for his opposite foot. One terrifying deep breath later, and he'd manoeuvred himself approximately half a metre closer to the top. Maybe he should stop measuring how far he'd climbed in half metres and start using full metres instead; after all, there were half as many of them. He shook that idea away. It was stupid, and he was starting to remind himself of Rocket. He might as well give up on everything the day he started thinking like her.

A sharp twinge stung the top of his head, and he reflexively let go of one hand to investigate. Out of the corner of his eye, a stone fell down below him, getting smaller and smaller until it disappeared out of sight completely. He swore at it.

Risking a look upwards to see what was going on, he was horrified to see Vale swinging from one hand, having lost her grip completely! If she wasn't in mortal danger, he'd chastise her for being complacent.

She slipped. More stones fell, but Galileo managed to dodge them. He screamed at her to hold on, but it was too late.

It felt like it was happening in slow motion, Vale's body flailing through the air, closer and closer to him. Before he knew it, she was adjacent to him and then beneath him. He reached out in a desperate attempt and grabbed onto a limb of some kind. The sudden increase in weight he was holding up nearly caused him to lose his grip as well. The friction on the tips of his fingers suddenly became unbearable. Vale smashed upside down into the rocks right below him with a thud, but she was safe… ish. His grip on her leg was the only thing keeping her from certain death.

Through all the strain that was happening to his body physically, his mind still took him back. Earlier that day—the *Leisurely Ländler* tilted practically on its side, caught in the storm and facing certain death. Leira was substituted for Vale, and an ocean of deadly waves was replaced by a drop into an ocean of trees. The same negative thoughts ran through his head, that of defeat and despair. *I can't hold on! I can't hold on!*

Vale came to the rescue, managing with some insane acrobatic skill to swing herself up to a position where she could grab back onto the wall and take some of the weight off him using him like a rope. He waited until she had a foothold before releasing her, quickly shaking the blood back into his aching arm.

'You okay?' he asked. Her stammered reply indicated she was, although visibly and audibly shaken. She'd probably have several bruises in the morning. She once again told him to get a shift on, although this time more sullenly, as if now just wanting the nightmare climb to be over and done with. This time, she proceeded behind him slower and more carefully.

Galileo practically crawled over the top before turning around to help Vale up the last couple of metres. They collapsed next to each other, both exhausted. Vale started laughing, completely illogically and inexplicably. She couldn't stop. She laughed so hard it was contagious, and he started laughing too!

She jumped up to her feet and opened her arms to the world, taking it all in. Galileo rolled onto his front and held up his face with his hands, looking out to the rest of the island, the ocean, the still singed *Ländler* and, finally, the sunset.

The silver sun continued setting towards the horizon, melting on the waves. Vale and Galileo said nothing, partly just watching in awe and partly exhausted after a day of walking and climbing. Galileo had set up a mat to the side on the stone surface of the plateau and covered it with his remaining rations for the day as well as a large scroll of parchment on which he'd drawn a rough sketch of the island. He'd detail it later from memory. *Objective completed.*

Other than the soft buzzing of the wild nightlife, the only sounds made were the occasional munches each of them would make when they ate a crispy pasmati cake.

'Shoot for the stars!' screamed Vale from nowhere, giving Galileo a good fright. 'That's the punchline! Now I just need to think of the joke.'

Galileo stared at her. She was lying on the ground, camera by her side, quill in hand and leaning a scroll of her own parchment on a rock. She turned her head to the floor, muttering an apology but failing to hide a grin before the scene returned to silence. Once again, it was Vale who broke it.

'Why did you come on this journey?'—munch. Galileo turned to her, waiting for an answer. Her legs swung casually in the air above her.

In the back of his mind, he wanted to have a go at her for ruining the beauty of the moment, for not appreciating where they were. Then he remembered she was only doing her job, the thing he'd asked her to do in the first place, so telling her off for that was simply not logical. Besides, he was quite capable of appreciating the view, eating snacks and answering questions at the same time. He thought about the answer. He could go into detail about the guild and the bullies, but he didn't quite feel ready to reveal that to the collective consciousness of her audience just yet, so for now decided to keep it simple.

'Art through knowledge, beauty through science, empiricism and idealism through rationalism, and reason through instinct.'— munch.

Vale scribbled along with him, concentrating on translating his words into what appeared to be a strange mixture of letters, numbers, and symbols. Galileo made a mental note to ask her about what he imagined was her own version of shorthand later. He'd love to have a go at writing poetry with it. Vale analysed the words she'd just written with a confused expression on her face.

'Could you be a little more specific?'—munch. It occurred to him that the audience she was writing for probably wouldn't want their articles to be written in riddles.

'I want to unleash the full potential and creativity of the human mind. Through creativity comes the desire to learn and gain knowledge. Creativity is intuition, and knowledge is rational, but it is the two combined that allow us to survive. The only option is for the two to work together. Where senses fail us, reason must step in.

Exploring and documenting the journey, *you* will kick-start a new "instinctivism" school of thought, which will revolutionise both science and art alike and propel *people* into the future.'—munch.

Vale continued to write as he spoke, concentrating hard on trying not to lose any of his meaning in the translation. A moment later, she raised her quill and turned back to him.

'What—' 'Why—' they said over each other, both stopping to let the other finish. Clearly not wishing to get into an awkward 'who should go first' scenario, Vale nodded at Galileo then lowered her head to let him go first.

'What about you?' he asked, nervously attempting to stretch his social muscles. Vale seemed surprised by the question. She was perhaps more used to being on the other end of the interview. Hopefully, this made a nice change for her. She put down the quill and looked out over the calm trees, the water, and the last vestiges of light from the sun and solemnly answered.

'I felt worthless in the City like I wasn't going anywhere, just static.' She sighed. 'You remember Mattai?'

Nod.

'We used to be friends. Then he got famous and left me behind. I've been trying to catch up ever since. Not to be on that level, but to overtake and to be better. Not for revenge, just for myself. To prove to myself that my life *was* worth something. To prove that I could. Stupid, really.' Galileo smiled. He could relate. 'As for the photography and the journalism, well… showing people that *their* lives are worth something beyond the City as well is a bonus.' She turned to him and smiled. 'Thank you for giving me the opportunity.'

'Thank you for exactly the same.'

And then the sun was gone.

They fell into silence once more, waiting until the darkness covered all the treetops below. Vale rolled the parchment away and got up and stared down at him, a look he interpreted as one that suggested they should find a way back down to Leira. He nodded, getting up himself.

'Should we take the revolving stairs or fly?' she asked with a deadpan expression.

Galileo thought about it, going through several advantages and disadvantages in his head of each of those. Flying would certainly be the quickest way back down, but it wasn't without its flaws. Vale burst out laughing.

'Oh,' he said, upset at himself for having fallen for the sarcasm. 'Oh,' he repeated, causing Vale to laugh harder. He stared down at his feet, shifting them back and forth awkwardly, his face burning red.

'Oh.'

Kalma reached the cliffs. There were signs that people had been here. Crumbled rocks and footsteps in the dust; she was right on their trail. She picked up a stone that seemed to have been dislodged from the rock-face to her left, crushing it in her hand and watching as the fragments fell to the ground. She looked around. *Where had they gone?*

But then she looked out towards the ocean. The sight of a ship spewing smoke stunned her. If this was the ship they'd arrived on, they must be rich indeed. What sort of treasures lay ripe for the taking in the holds of that vessel? Well, there was only one way to find out. She'd collect her traps later. She pressed a button on the side of her helmet, and her vision narrowed and focused on the ship. It was very far away, but she could clearly make out a figure on deck, who appeared to be hanging upside down from the top of the crow's nest, swinging wildly out of control, quickly hammering something into a mast when gravity happened to navigate them towards it. A builder? An artificer?

She prepared her bow and aimed at the person on the ship. She swayed her arms to keep the figure in her cross-hairs as they moved, knowing that the aim-assist would account for the offset. Just a release of tension, and they'd have an arrow through their skull. Easy.

She sheathed. It was too risky. Not only might she alert more people, but they might hold important information. How many more people are were there? Where were the treasures? She could force them to tell her how to sail the ship, and take the whole thing for herself. Now *that* was an enticing thought. Between the reptile and the ship, this was looking to be her lucky day.

The Hungry Gamins

The sound of sirens waning in the distance woke Tawney up. A shame too, she'd been having such a lovely dream about... about... well damned if she could remember, but she was sure it was great. *Oh, come on. Five more minutes.* How could they still be looking for her so many hours into the night and so long after the fact?

Her eyes opened to the sight of an alleyway, not the one she last remembered seeing, but dark and dingy all the same. The last few hours of consciousness were a mad blur of fading memories. She had no idea where she was, only that it was somewhere in The Snickets. Somehow it felt like a million years since she'd been running over the rooftops and through the streets. Her entire body ached with bruises, but she forced herself up, lamenting the pile of flattened wicker baskets she appeared to have used as a bed.

She took a moment to consider how far she'd come. From the dungeons to Ash's penthouse and practically everything in between, yet she was still not free. She had to somehow get past those patchwork metal walls that kept the outsiders out, trapping her inside the City like a bronzefish in a net.

Giving her brain another minute to start properly functioning, she mentally went through some of the options she had at getting past the wall:

Option 1: Below. If she could somehow dig deep enough to get under the wall, she could then dig back up the other side. Advantages: No Blue Guard. Disadvantages: Slow; risk of being buried alive, something that she didn't wish to happen again; requires some kind of digging contraption. She put a pin in that one for now.

Option 2: Straight through the middle. If she could find a section of the wall that was unguarded, she may be able to find a way of cutting through. Advantages: Low risk of death; quick. Disadvantages: Leaves a highly visible trace; requires some kind of cutting tool. It seemed more feasible than option 1, but was there anything better?

Option 3: Above. This one would involve finding a building of approximately the same height as the wall and testing the jumping skills she'd honed over the last day or so. Advantages: Quick, no special tools required, only agility. Disadvantages: She would be visible, and those barbed wood-wire spikes on the top would make one hell of a nasty landing.

No option was perfect, but none entirely mitigated the risk of the entire journey being for nothing. She had to choose, and option three required the least preparation, and being honest with herself, she just wanted to get the hell out of the City as fast as she could. If she ended up looking like a block of eyed cheese, so be it.

'Can we help you miss?!' came an angry high-pitched voice from behind her. Startled, she turned to face a group of children, clothed in a tattered mish-mash of garments. The leader of the group, black-skinned, covered in dirt, and no more than eleven years old, threatened Tawney's person with a primitively sharpened stick. It was at this point that she realised the wicker basket she'd flattened in her sleep had likely belonged to one of them. Indeed, she was probably encroaching on their territory. Well then, time to show them who's boss. She was itching to be in control of something again.

'Who are you?' she asked quickly, accusingly, and with authority, 'Snicket guards?' The girl was confused, a question which she had not expected. She turned to her mates as Tawney waited for a reply.

'We're the Gamins, ain't we. Everyone knows who we are, though no one talks about it, mind you. They ain't allowed.' The girl moved in closer with the stick. 'We keep to the side streets, out of sight and out of mind. Now you!'

Tawney introduced herself, slowly walking nearer to the girl as she did so, making herself as large and intimidating as possible.

The girl edged backwards, subconsciously retracting the stick. Once she was near enough, Tawney stopped telling her story and swiped at the stick, knocking it out of her hands and onto the ground. Quickly, she trapped it under her foot before the girl could pick it up again.

'You had me worried there for a sec,' she said condescendingly, picking the stick up herself and turning her back, faking a yawn as if she was about to go back to sleep. She kicked the basket. 'Never liked children.'

'Oy! That belongs to Tyger,' she said, gesturing to a boy of around half her size, cowering behind her. 'You gonna replace that for him, *Grasshead?!*' Tawney knew the girl had meant it as an insult about her hair, but she kinda liked it. Tawney smirked and strode up to her. Looking down, the older girl walked around the younger one, both circling each other like two hunters, each trying to stalk the other out.

'Disarmed and still making threats, are you? How dumb can you get? Ah, you're pathetic you lot, ain't ya?' she sneered with a sudden lurch forward, giving the Gamin leader a good shock at the same time just to keep her on her toes. 'You're lodging-less,' she said, subtly kicking the remains of the basket again. 'You're dirty,' she said, flicking strands of the kid's locks through her hands, promptly met with an aggressive swat. 'You're hungry… and quite frankly, you smell like a farmer milked the wrong end of a wood-bovine.' Tawney just hoped the kids weren't witty enough to point out that she, too, was all of the things she was accusing them of.

They were silent, thankfully. 'Alright, I'll do you a deal. You help me. I help you. How's that sound?'

'We ain't helping you, Grasshead! You're one of them citizens.'

'Do I look like a citizen to you? Does you think I'd be down here if I was a citizen? Citizens never come down into The Snickets, do they?' Tawney said, imitating their childish tone. The leader thought about it, turning to the rest of her gang for guidance. One of them nodded hesitantly before she turned back.

'What you got for us?' she asked.

Tawney explained her plan. Knowledge for knowledge. After correctly assuming they got what they did by simply asking nicely, she offered to show them how to steal food, clothes, and everything they could need to survive and not get caught in the process. They, in turn, would help her escape the City. She explained her three options: dig under, cut through, or jump over. A voice towards the back of the gang piped up.

'We know where you can find cutting tools! There's a—' the voice was interrupted by a groan, and a boy at the back recoiling from an elbow which a girl to his left had applied to his stomach. Tawney's strategy changed in her mind in light of the cards the boy had accidentally shown her. She knew they had the information she wanted, and she was gonna get it. The leader thanked the girl at the back for not ruining the deal further and turned to re-face Tawney, spitting on the palm of her hand and holding it out, facing upwards.

'Zauré. Nice to meet you.'

Tawney felt like a general ordering around the Gamins, placing them in position around the perimeter of the bakers, hiding down the narrow alleys by the side, keeping to the shadows. By now, the sun was rising, and the clouds were clearing, the surrounding atmosphere sharp, biting and cold to the skin. This early in the morning, it was unlikely there'd be people walking about, but the shop workers would wake up early so that loaves, rum-buns, and all manner of tasty treats would be freshly baked for the freshly woken rush-hour crowd.

'Found it!' came a loud whisper from nearby. Tawney and Zauré ducked down together beneath the level of the half-open windows of the bakery and made their way towards the voice. The kid was excitedly pointing through the window, and sure enough, there was the main kitchen area they'd been hunting for. At present, a lone worker inside prepared today's special pastries on a flour-covered table and extracted trays from a metal stove that were covered in sugar-glazed custarts. Tawney's stomach rumbled. She was mostly doing this for the Gamins, but, oh boy, if that didn't look appealing, then nothing did. Trying to work out how much time had passed since her last night in the cell was nigh on impossible. Hours? Days?

'What do we do now?' Zauré asked.

It was all on Tyger. Tawney hoped that he didn't lose his nerve. She was confident and nervous all at once. The thrill of stealing food was returning, but she was used to doing it on her own.

A moment later, a nervous Tyger appeared through the door at the front of the shop, hesitantly ringing the bell on the counter and tentatively looking around. *Come on, Tyger. Stay cool. Follow the script.* The worker greeted him, and he put on a cute face.

'Now!'

With the target distracted, Tawney lifted the window so that it was fully open. One by one, the five-strong remainder of the gang filed in quietly. As planned, they formed a human daisy chain, transferring the fresh treats from their trays all the way along to the end where Zauré collected them in a sack.

Tawney, whilst holding the heavier than expected window open, kept an eye on Tyger, and more importantly, the worker. She got more and more nervous the longer they took. A twitch here, a rub of the neck there. There were signs of boredom, subtle indications that they wanted to get back to their job that her hunting instincts helped her spot. It didn't help that Tyger kept glancing over towards her. Was he looking for validation of performing his part correctly? Was he just nervous? Who knew?

Her eyes wandered nervously towards the worktop, on which lay the latest issue of City, The Curious. She tilted her head to read the headlines: '*Everything is Perfect,*' '*Crime rate finally reaches 0%,*' '*Šéf granted special powers to—,*' but a bread roll covered the end of that sentence. She frowned. What sort of news articles were they? Where had all the good journalists gone? Crime rate at zero percent? *We'll see about that.*

Without warning, the worker turned around, his expression of calm but tired turning to shocked in a moment.

'Run!' screamed Tawney. The kid at the end of the line dropped the treats back onto the tray and dashed for the window.

Unfortunately, he was met by a queue of his comrades also trying to escape. *If only there were more windows.* It was then that she realised that there were, in fact, more windows. *If only there were more of me to open the other windows.*

The worker dashed back into the main kitchen, grabbing on to the last kid in the queue just as he was about to climb through. The kid screamed, kicking his legs wildly. Tawney shoved out a girl who was climbing and went inside herself.

Without even thinking, she tackled the worker to the floor, took a fist to his head and tore the kid off him, pinning the innocent baker down. Pointing him at the window, she gave the Gamin a few seconds to escape before releasing the worker and departing via the window herself, violently banging shut the window behind her so that the man couldn't follow her through. She quickly looked back through it, but the baker was still lying on the ground and didn't appear to be moving.

'Split up, meet back at Tyger's basket! Go!' she ordered. The Gamins obeyed, but Tawney held back Zauré by the scruff of the collar. 'Alright, now where's them cutting tools?'

'You kiddin'? After that?! I'm not telling you nothing, lady.'

'I did what we agreed, tell me!'

'They're gonna have the Blue Guard after them any minute, and it's all your fault!' Zauré retaliated. The Gamin leader tried to escape to run after her gang, but Tawney lifted the girl to her face, her legs desperately kicking at thin air. 'Let me go, Grasshead! You're crazy!'

'I did what we agreed, didn't I? You lil' idiots just need a little practice, don't you? Now, tell me where I can find them cutting tools.'

Tawney looked dead into Zauré's eyes. The girl was terrified. Not of the baker, not even of the Blue Guard. *She* was the scariest thing right now.

'Th... the... there's an abandoned workshop, right on the other side of the City near the wall. It's on one of them farms. Supposed to belong to some artificer type. We overheard the Blue Guard talking about raiding it, but you might find something.'

Tawney let Zauré free. She ran off down the alley without a second thought, leaving Tawney alone.

The same sirens she'd woken up to earlier that morning echoed off the walls. *Oh Tawney, what have you done?* Stolen from and assaulted an innocent baker and outlawed a bunch of lodging-less children is what she'd done. In the fight for survival, there were no rules. She'd survived being the prey for so long she could feel herself starting to become the predator. What sort of monster hunts hungry children?

She looked down at her knuckles, the skin bruised and torn slightly where she'd punched an innocent man. She rubbed them, a physical reminder that she wasn't Tawney anymore. *Tawney wouldn't hurt a luminon.* She needed a new name for herself. The Gamins' one seemed fitting.

If the town of Runaway still existed, she'd have tried to get the Gamins there. It would have been the perfect place for them. The old Sheriff and the town doctor would have looked after them for sure. Lots of conflicting emotions happened on her face.

Feeling confused, afraid, and ashamed of herself, she ran back into darkness.

Grasshead found herself in a field, just outside a small wooden hut, surrounded by exceptionally large blades of grass, which clawed at her tattered and torn, blood-dried dungeon clothing. *Someone really ought to mow this*, she thought to herself. The hut seemed abandoned. The windows were smashed, the roof half falling in, and the door swinging in the wind on its hinges. A lantern inside flickered at random intervals. Whoever was there last had forgotten to turn the lights off or had been in too much of a hurry to do so.

She approached the door and scanned it up and down. Dozens of broken locks hung on the inside; *someone was paranoid.* As she stepped through, carefully avoiding the broken glass on the floor, she heard a noise. Just for a moment, but definitely there.

Three blood ravens were flying directly at her, terrifyingly sharp claws poised to strike. She ducked, but the birds ignored her, instead escaping past her through the door, flying up and away into the sky.

Her attention returned to the workshop. She looked around. The place had been almost completely ransacked. The only thing left standing was a large contraption made of rusted metal cogs attached to the wall. This had clearly been the workshop of a great inventor. She wondered what had happened to them.

All the deathly feelings she'd felt in the City seemed amplified in this place. Her senses told her not to continue. If she wasn't so desperate to find something that would help her escape the City, there's no way she'd have gone any further, but she was in so deep now there was no turning back.

She closed her eyes and focused her instincts, hoping to pick up anything that might tell her about what had happened here. When she opened her eyes, the tables were covered in blueprints, the walls covered in tools, the ceiling with inventions, and the gentle hum of engines rung through the air—sensory images of the past.

She walked to the table and looked over the blueprint parchments. The first thing that struck her was the terrible handwriting on each and every single one of them. She looked at the first one. It was a design for a flying vehicle that looked remarkably similar to the drones she'd been chased by. She looked at another, a design for a combination of objects: a mast with a speaker on the top, hauntingly similar to the one she'd used against the Blue Guard on the rooftop, and a personal radio device to go with it. The title had mostly faded away, but she could just about make out the word 'Behaviour.'

The final piece of parchment actually had a legible title—'*The Leisurely Ländler.*' Its scale and ambition were clearly the designs of a raving lunatic. It was a curious thing, like a normal ship but massive and with enormous cylinders on the base. The author had indicated that they were to shoot fire. But the weirdest thing about it was the large mast in the middle, drawn in dotted lines. At the top of the mast were attached yet more jet engines and little arrows that indicated that they should spin to keep the vehicle more stable. It reminded her of something. It took a moment for her to realise that if she turned the *Leisurely Ländler* on its side, then the spinning engines at the top would look exactly like the spider drones themselves. Indeed, placing the blueprints of each side by side, they were almost identical. Could the designs for this ship, the *Leisurely Ländler* have been adapted from the spiders or vice versa?

Things were starting to make a little more sense, although still not completely. Perhaps this had been the workshop of an inventor who worked for the Blue Guard or the Order of the City? Or, perhaps the Blue Guard had raided this place and then used the designs to build their own spider drones and 'behaviour' masts? If the latter was true, how would they know to raid it, and why? Something didn't quite add up.

But she was getting distracted. The place felt creepy and had a deathly aura, even this far out on the edge of the City. She just needed to find some kind of cutting tool and get the hell out. To that end, she re-adjusted her instincts and the images of the past faded away; only the torn edges of the parchments survived, rendered illegible from a thin coating of dust.

Something glimmered in the corner of her senses, like a flame. She walked over to the corner, moving an empty cabinet and revealing a secret compartment that even the Blue Guard had missed, and inside, a blowtorch, amongst other more dangerous tools. *Perfect*. But why hide them at all? It was almost as though whoever worked here had expected to be raided—more and more questions about this place.

But Grasshead had what she needed. Without putting too much extra thought into it, she grabbed the blowtorch and escaped this cursed place.

It took her several hours to return to the main part of the City and find a relatively unguarded but well-hidden section of the wall. It didn't help that she was trying to avoid being spotted by literally everyone. She was on the run from the Blue Guard, the Gamins, the citizens, and even from herself. *You can always judge a woman by the quality of her enemies.*

Trying to work out how this tool actually operated was a pretty decent distraction, though. After laying out the torch on the floor, she realised that it was supposed to be wearable, so she lifted it over her head and dropped it on like a harness. There were so many buttons and so many orifices; she didn't want to kill herself accidentally. After locating a panel on the base with three icons: a flame, a lightning bolt and a peculiar mesh that seemed infinite in its designs, she pointed the main nozzle at the wall and pressed the flame one.

Nothing happened. She cranked a handle on the side.

The sudden knock-back almost blew her off her feet, but after she steadied herself and forced down her feet, she moved the nozzle closer to the wall, continuing to wind the lever as she did so. The rusted silver became red hot instantly. Slowly, a divot appeared, and she knew it was working. The rest of the process was painfully slow and loud. Every few seconds, she looked over her shoulder to make sure no one was coming, but eventually, she had cut around an area big enough to duck under. All that was left to do was kick out the metal there, and then she'd be free.

Not wanting to wait any longer, she stopped winding and released the button. She took a run up, raising her foot and making contact with the centre of the cut area, not even bothering to check that it had cooled down first. Her soles were so blistered already that it didn't matter anyway; she didn't feel a thing.

The sunlight shined through. Freedom. Nothing but the desert laid out in front of her, devoid of everything but sand, yet still somehow feeling less deathly than the City. She didn't realise how much she'd missed this sight—to stare out at something natural. It was heavenly.

There was something nearby: danger. She felt it.

A Blue Guard patrolling the outer wall jolted towards her. Thinking quick, Grasshead twisted herself round and pointed the blowtorch at the guard, tapping the lightning bolt icon on the base and rapidly winding the lever. Sparks shot out of the front and engulfed the guard in electricity like it was trapped in a net. Just as before, the guard gyrated and vibrated with the shock frantically before falling over backwards into the sand. Now they knew where she was, and they'd once again be hot on her tail, but this time she was one step closer and had a way to fight back.

The sand stretched out over the horizon. Somewhere beyond it was Runaway, and somewhere beyond that was the forest. She was thirsty and starving. If she could get to her old town, she may be able to find some food or water there before continuing on. Not looking back, Grasshead ran out of the shadows and into the light.

Rocket shivered. A feeling flowed through her, the kind of feeling you get when someone walks over your grave or goes into your bedroom without your permission. Her repairs and improvements were nearly complete, and her beautiful ship was just about ready to leave. She walked up to the helm and was about to lift off before realising that the rest of her crew were yet to return from exploring the tropical island. She looked up at the mast she'd just installed and the array of engines there—her 'spalancer' as she called it. It spun and helped with balance, so the name made perfect sense.

It felt like they'd been gone for ages. She'd thought through the things she'd done in her head: built the spalancer, repaired the fire and water damage, fixed Leira's winged earpiece, configured six different flavours of bathwater, and even created a few *extra* special surprises for the crew upon their return. Now she was bored.

Rocket sighed. She could burn down the sails again? Nah, the others might think it was some kind of emergency flare. She was too awake to sleep, and the intense heat from the descending sun didn't help with that.

There was only one thing for it. Rocket stepped down from the helm and went below deck, walking down the corridor past Leira and Veroushka's room, past Galileo's and past Vale's, finally stopping outside the door to Doc Holliday's cabin. She grabbed the handle, twisted it, and opened the door. She got what she needed and returned to the deck.

The hours passed. At least, they felt like hours. There was still no sign of her crew. It was quiet out here, only the gentle lapping of the waves against the freshly mended hull of the *Ländler* kept her company. Too quiet. Even the birds seemed to have stopped chirping.

Rocket walked over to the edge and leant over the railing, peering into the strangely sparkling water. It was clear blue, yet eerily still. The lapping of the waves had stopped; there weren't even any ripples.

She narrowed her eyes, focusing deep down. Something glinted. Whatever it was, it was rapidly rising to the surface. Before she knew what was happening, a figure leapt up out of the ocean, giving her an eyeful of bronze armour, before a sharp pain on the back of her head caused everything to go black.

Sleeping Bounty

Rocket's eyes snapped open to the sight of a green material. The seams that ran along it informed her that this was some kind of tent. Her head hurt, and it felt like she was propped up against something hard. *Don't panic yet. This might not be a bad thing,* she told herself. Trying to get up, she found her hands had been tied around a wooden pole with a length of thick rope, the same pole she was propped up against.

Rocket imagined possible scenarios that might involve being tied to a pole with rope, trying to figure out if this was a good or bad situation to be in. After playing out a few, she decided that there was simply not enough evidence to tell at the current moment in time.

The place was littered with carcasses and bags of hunting supplies, but the inhabitant was absent. Rocket felt grateful that she'd lost her sense of smell thanks to an argument that had once taken place between her nostrils and a ball of flames—her nostrils had won. It probably reeked of sweat and death in here.

The flaps of the tent entrance opened, and Rocket squinted the sun away before getting a good look at the woman who had walked in. She was imposing, had short, light hair, and wore shining bronze armour from neck to toe. This was starting to look like it might be a good situation after all; at least, it was somewhat similar to one of the positive scenarios she'd imagined.

'Where's the treasure?' she asked, smiling condescendingly. Naturally, Rocket had no idea what she was talking about.

'You're looking at it,' Rocket grinned back. An elbow introduced itself to her cheek. *Okay, not good.*

'Who else are you here with?'

Rocket did her best to look pensive.

'Are you scared of me or something? 'Cos there are only a finite number of reasons I can think of for tying someone up like this, and this isn't one I was hoping for.' Another elbow said hello to her other cheek. Rocket had never liked symmetry or the taste of blood. She confessed they were a group of explorers, that she was an inventor, and also their captain.

The woman approached, planting her feet on either side of Rocket's legs, squatting over her to meet her face to face.

'You don't... happen to have a girl with blue hair with you?' she asked. Why did Rocket get the feeling that she already knew the answer? Was there any use lying? She'd promised Holliday she'd protect Leira. It didn't matter. She'd hesitated too much, and the truth was obvious. Her captor's metal armour clunked as she stood back up again, smirked, turned her back on Rocket, and headed towards the exit.

'See you later, hun. I'm going out hunting. When I get back, I'm eager to hear one of those reasons for tying someone up you *were* hoping for, eh?'

The sun blinded Rocket as the tent opened. When it was closed again, her captor had gone.

She knew it. She'd read that handsome captain like a book.

That girl, sitting all alone in the glade, ignorantly singing to herself, definitely had blue highlights in her hair. Shame too, she seemed so sweet and innocent, but once she handed her over to the Guard, she'd never see her again. The smell of the Honeywax she'd get from this was sweet indeed.

Kalma balanced at her spot in the trees, hidden from view as the girl laid down on top of the wall, formulating a plan of attack and mentally going through her options:

Option 1: Above. She could drop down out of the trees and capture her before she realised what was happening. Advantages: Quick and clean. Disadvantages: It was still light, just about. Now she knew that it hadn't just been the cowboy and the marionette here on the island. If there were others nearby, she didn't want to risk alerting them.

Option 2: Through the arch of thorns. She'd wait till nightfall and simply walk in under the cover of darkness. Hopefully, she'd fall asleep soon. Advantages: Less likely to be spotted, no resistance. Disadvantages: Relies on the girl still being there in an hour's time, and besides, it was far less fun. For the price offered, however, she wasn't going to take any chances.

She didn't know how much time had passed, but the quantity of light seeping through the branches was eventually minimal enough to be well hidden. After stretching her muscles and rolling her head around to kick-start her body back into gear, she slid down the branch, landing silently on the leafy ground just a few footsteps from the archway. It formed a border around the girl as she slept peacefully on the wall next to the waterfall like the frame to some ancient painting. As she crept towards her, the hunter hoped that, like a normal teenager, she'd be able to sleep through anything. *All alone, oblivious, and mine!*

Suddenly, her body was thrown to the side with great force, and she felt herself being pinned down to the floor. Claws scratched at her armour from head to toe. Above her towered a ferocious creature. The llama-bear was twice her size, covered in burgundy hair and snarling at her as it reared on its hind legs, stretching its long neck towards her face and giving her a good view of its vicious teeth.

Kalma reached over her shoulder for her bow, but her hands failed to grip anything. A quick glance to the floor beside the animal confirmed that it must have torn it off her. It lay painfully out of reach. *Stay calm... and still...*

The animal returned to all fours and stared at her, blocking the path into the glade. Was it *protecting* the girl? *Why would it do that?* She slowly skirted around to the left, attempting to see if there was any way to bypass the archway, and picked up her bow along the way. Was it smart enough to know it was a weapon?

The thing lurched forward at her again with a growl. Without having time to prepare the bow, she grabbed an arrow from its holster and stabbed it into the creature's neck. It swiped at her, making contact with her bronze helmet and knocking her back into a bush before it reeled and howled in pain from the arrow.

Now with time, she prepared her bow with an arrow and aimed at the wounded animal, but before she could fire, she caught movement out of the corner of her eye. Lowering the bow, she realised she was completely surrounded by wildlife. All sorts of creatures circled her, moving in closer, walls of snarls trapping her like a critter in a net or a pet in a cage. Big, small, flying, walking, purple, green, hairy, scaled, four-legged, eight-legged... twenty-legged! Blue circlets flashed in front of her eyes, obscuring her vision. She switched her aim between the animals frantically, from a deer-like creature to two small yellow birds. No way did she have enough arrows for all of them. Nor enough time.

She knew when she was beaten. Kalma turned on the spot and dashed. The wild pack chased. She clicked her heels together, feeling the force of their jets build. Her feet left the ground, and for a moment, she thought she'd escaped, but a claw wrapped itself around her greaves and brought her back down again. The flames exploded from her soles and scorched the creature, but it didn't matter.

The hunter was helpless as the alliance of angry animals tore at her...

It was getting darker, and they were so close to giving up. Holliday was tired and hungry, and he was sure Veroushka knew it. But if they didn't get this hunter, it would play on both their minds forever. He didn't want that for either of them. Sadly, nobody had attempted to kill him over the last hour or so, so it was possible that they'd left the island altogether or had mastered the art of vanishing.

Eventually, they stumbled upon a clearing. Just a small one, but there was a tent pitched in the middle and weapons leaning against a tree to the side. This could only be the hunter's base.

Holliday went first, keeping as low as he could and hiding in the bushes in case they were still there. Veroushka grabbed onto his arm before he walked into the middle, warning him to be careful. He drew his revolver and forward-rolled into the clearing, springing up at the tent entrance and aiming right at it. He grabbed onto the zip and pulled it down quickly.

'And it's about time too!' said Rocket, tugging on her bonds to incite Holliday into freeing her. His face must have been a sight. With one of the hunting knives lying on the ground, he cut the ropes as she explained how she'd got there.

He looked around further. What he saw was a lot, even for him —dead animals and their skins everywhere. Slabs of meat rested against a makeshift stove. The smell was rotten. Some of them were so small and common even in the City; they couldn't be worth anything. No, whoever was doing this wasn't just doing it for money; they were doing it for fun. What they didn't kill for fun or entertainment, Holliday imagined, would be sold illegally on the black market in the City. It wasn't just the invasive scent making him feel sick.

He called Veroushka over, telling her it was safe, but warned her that she might not want to go inside the tent, at which she reminded him that she could not smell smells. She didn't appreciate his attempts to shelter her further, and regardless of how much the sight may upset her, she was sure the experience would do her good. Cynical, he held open the tent for her as her strings guided her in.

'*C'est mal...* ' she whispered under her breath, doing her best to hide her distress but failing miserably. The paint around her eyes seemed to mar slightly. 'Rocket! What are you doing here?'

'Having a picnic.'

'You got the stuff?' Holliday asked the marionette, helping up Rocket and guiding her out of the tent.

'*Oui,*' she whimpered, showing him the glass pouch of berries.

'Then do what you gotta do and make it quick.'

Veroushka nodded, and Holliday left with Rocket to hide amidst the trees. Holliday explained what she was doing and why —coating the weapons and the rations in diluted mortazine to knock out the dangerous hunter, who had been murdering everything on the island. When she had completed her task, Veroushka joined them in the trees. Holliday prayed that their plan would work.

'We have the island on our side, *mon ami.* The poison will do its job. Besides, from what you've told me about your biology, they will have to eat eventually!'

He was actually surprised she'd been listening to him. But just as Holliday was about to praise her for it, she tugged on his clothing, urging him to duck lower.

Without warning, Rocket dashed out from cover and back towards the tent. Holliday reached to grab her, but she was too quick.

'Rocket!' he shouted in a whisper. But before he could give chase, he caught a familiar glimpse of the hunter's bronze power-armour. He gritted his teeth as Rocket disappeared inside. *What was she doing?*

As the hunter staggered in, they removed their helmet, finally revealing to him what the mysterious hunter looked like: short-cropped hair, scar down her left cheek and covered in bruises. That, combined with the multitude of scratch marks on her previously gleaming bronze armour, she looked in a rough way.

He was ashamed of himself for having expected her to be male. He imagined the scorning Sheriff Eliza would have given him. It hurt, yet he wished he could've heard it. Maybe capturing this hunter would somehow remedy his past mistakes. There was some logic there, he hoped... and doubted.

'Elle est mal...'

It felt like the hunter was doing everything she could to avoid going in the tent: hanging her helmet on a branch, taking off her compound bow and quiver to lean them against the trunk of a tree, but there was no way she could know of the trap they'd laid.

Eventually, after the tension became almost unbearable, she finally headed inside. Holliday shared a knowing glance with Veroushka, each as hopeful as the other that the marionette's plan was working, but neither knowing for sure. What was going on in there? He hoped Rocket knew what she was doing.

After an eternity of waiting, finally, the hunter reappeared, stumbling out of the tent, eyes darting around wildly, and a look of sheer fright plastered onto her face. She spun round in circles, attempting to grab her bow, eventually catching it with her hand and the arrows with her other. She fired up in the air and in all directions wildly.

Holliday couldn't help but feel slightly sorry for her, having an idea of the kind of horror that she might be going through and the visions that the island was placing in her head. But the plan was working, and she'd no longer be a threat to the island or his friends.

A storm of dead birds and bloody arrows fell from the sky all around. Eventually, when she had run out of arrows, she threw the bow to the floor and charged straight into a tree, knocking herself out and falling flat on the ground. For someone who had demonstrated strength way above what Doc Holliday thought humans were capable of, suddenly, she didn't seem quite so threatening.

Veroushka headed straight for the poor animals that had been unlucky enough to be caught in the cross-fire whilst Holliday headed for the tent, nearly colliding into Rocket as she vacated the premises, holding her rope. Holliday was dumbfounded. She dropped the rope to the floor and shrugged.

'She'd have known something was up if I wasn't there...'

He looked over her muscled body lying on the ground and dreaded the thought of carrying it back down to the beach and how many return trips he'd have to make for her... belongings. He could tie her up now and wait for her to wake, but he really didn't know how long she'd be out for. Actually, that was a good point. He pressed a thumb against her and felt relieved to feel the regular pulse.

It took several attempts and Rocket's help to get her over his shoulders; it was at times like this he wished he had his trusty mechanical horse. By the time they'd managed it, Veroushka was by his side. She shook her head miserably; there was nothing to be done for the birds that had fallen.

Leira wondered at what point she should start getting worried. She didn't quite know how long she'd been here for. By now, it was pretty much completely dark, the only light being the rising moons reflecting off the sparkling water. *Phew, can't have been too long.*

She considered trying to head back to the beach by herself, but what if Vale and Galileo came looking for her? Besides, she was in no hurry to leave. It seemed like the place would be fairly warm at night, she could probably construct some primitive shelter out of branches, and the various berries and fruits she'd seen dangling up amidst the leaves were *probably* edible, going from what Holliday had taught her, at least.

Suddenly feeling immensely tired, Leira laid herself down on the rock wall, curling up as tightly as she could. Although it wasn't as comfortable as her bed on the ship, somehow, it was softer than both prior lodgings—both her home in the City and Holliday's surgery in Runaway. Within minutes, she was asleep.

The sound of laughter woke her up, which was a shame because she'd been having such a lovely dream about light refraction, although she was sure she'd heard several wild animals snarling at some point. She wanted so badly to know more from Galileo. His words had clearly made an impact, so much so that the magic of science had invaded her imaginary night-vision.

She hauled up her head and looked around the glade. The laughter was faint, but the glade was empty. She concentrated hard on the noise and realised it was coming from above her.

Forcing herself off the comfort of the wall, she tried to locate the source. Left a bit. No... right a bit... right a bit more. She climbed over the wall and waded through the water towards the waterfall. The sound was coming from on top of it!

'Hello?' she shouted up. The laughter stopped, replaced by a rustling in the bushes. Then, a face appeared, one Leira recognised. Vale smiled down at her. 'What are you doing up there?!'

'Leira! Thank goodness you're still okay. We must have come all the way around in a circle,' she said as Galileo appeared next to her.

Leira eyed up the waterfall, it was probably thirty foot or so high, not low enough to jump safely, and the water below was nowhere near deep enough to break the fall sufficiently.

'Is there any way you can climb down?' she shouted up at them.

Vale and Galileo looked at each other as their smiles vanished.

Last of the Runaways

The hot sand burnt the soles of her feet and the palms of her hands as Grasshead crawled back through the entrance of the town. Although she had barely enough strength left in her eyes to keep them open, she could just make out the welcome sign by her side, incorrectly stating the population of Runaway as 31. She crossed her eyes, blurring out the '3' and instantly regretting it.

Seven hours running, then walking and then on all fours through the intense heat of the sun with nowhere to rest for shelter had drained her of hope and energy.

She dragged herself through the automatic electronic gates to the tavern, around the bodies of some fallen Blue Guard and discarded the elemental blowtorch on the bar-top, shifting the corpse of the barmaid to one side. She hauled herself into the kitchen and lifted herself up, stuck her head under the sink, thankful that the plumbing in the town was still functional as burning hot water poured into her mouth. Not bothering to turn the thing off, she collapsed on the hard floor.

She woke up unable to breathe, but after a moment of panic, coughing and spluttering, realised she was only drowning in the water which the sink had failed to capture. She got up off the floor, twisted off the tap and splashed back through to the main room of the tavern, this time able to assess the destruction. She closed the barmaid's eyes, picked up her body and took it out into the street, carrying it into a building on the other side.

A mixture of wooden boxes lined the walls, a worktop in the centre contained planks, strips of metal and various tools. She placed the body into one of the caskets and lifted that into the street, went back inside for a shovel, and dug. The repetitive motion of lifting and pressing the end of the shovel into the sand was cathartic. It gave her time to think and plan. She'd spend the day searching the town for any food, drink and medical supplies that hadn't been looted already. She could afford a day, surely.

Pressing against the side of the casket, it finally fell into the hole. She recited a prayer for her friend before beginning the gruelling task of covering it with the sand she'd just dug up.

Grasshead loathed herself and what she'd become, replaying the scenes of her own violence in her mind and wishing she could have found another way. Tawney would never hurt a luminon, but Grasshead did whatever it took to survive, no matter the cost.

Tawney faced her problems with words and wit, but Grasshead faced hers...

The sound of the shots she'd taken at the guards on the roof rang through her head like a siren. Suddenly, she remembered that she was still wearing Ash's holster, and in it, her revolver and a small pouch of bullets. She placed a finger on it, but it felt hot to the touch, and she whisked her hand away.

Why do I want to survive so bad? What's in it for me? It was like some kind of built-in process that she couldn't shut off no matter how hard she tried; it was driving her insane. Survival at *all costs*. It was exhausting. What's the point when everyone's out to hunt you?

The grave was complete, and Grasshead returned to the tavern, looking inside the coolers and compartments for any scraps of food. She ran her hands over some Honeywax coins on the top, pocketing them. She found two packs of roasted tater-nuts and downed both of them in seconds. Somehow, they only made her hungrier.

Next stop, the surgery. She hunted through Doc Holliday's cupboards but found nothing except an aura of despair. It made her angry, full of blame and hatred and things she didn't understand, as if everything she'd been through and everything she'd done had started here. Her instincts told her to get out, so she ran back through the electric metal doors onto the street and felt calmer instantly, confused as to what had just happened.

Once more, Grasshead returned to the tavern. Once more, the exhaustion hit. Judging from the position of the sun, either she hadn't slept on the kitchen floor for long, or she'd slept an entire day already. She guessed and hoped that it was the former. She squelched over to the stairs and went up to find a room, crashing out on the first bed she came across. It was the comfiest thing in existence. Finally, a proper rest. She was out within seconds and went to sleep dreaming of the eternal forest.

Tomorrow.

Stomp. Stomp. Stomp.

Grasshead'd been woken in her sleep so many times over the last couple of days that she'd almost built up a resistance to it—adapted to her surroundings. Only this time, it was probably not the best course of action to survive.

Stomp. Stomp... Crash!

The sudden sound shocked Grasshead fully awake. The faint glimmer of blue she knew was unnatural in the desert, but it took a moment for her brain gears to kick in to realise that the figure was pointing a musket at her and that her life was once again in danger.

Grasshead rolled to the side, grabbing hold of the bedsheets and falling onto the wooden floor as the first of the guard's shots obliterated the bed. Scrambling up as the guard reloaded, she threw the sheet over it and leapt for the top of the door frame, swinging herself forwards feet first and kicking the guard out of the room as it shot a second round into the ceiling. It stumbled backwards and fell over the railing, annihilating a table and finally landing onto the soaked floor of the tavern.

Looking down, three more guards inhabited the lower level. Not bothering with the cumbersome stairs, she jumped over the railing and landed on the bar-top, kicking down a guard that tried to grab onto her as she picked up the blowtorch and quickly slipped it on.

She pointed the nozzle down at the floor, tapped the lightning bolt icon and rapidly wound it up. A storm began spreading over the entire water-coated surface, showing no mercy for all four guards that were caught up in its relentless prongs, screaming.

Her brain told her it was time to let go, but her hands refused to comply. She stood and stared at the floor as they continued to be electrocuted. Then, they stopped screaming. The electric tornado continued to flood through them, their muscular reflexes still gyrating in response to the energy, but there was no question about it; they were dead. Even then, she still couldn't stop.

It was only the machine strapped around her body running out of fuel that caused the bombardment to cease. The last guard stopped moving, and the last sparks died away. The place was deadly silent, and Grasshead hated every second sound waves failed to collide with her eardrums.

More Blue Guard burst through the tavern's doors, tearing the metal from its hinges and taking aim at her. She jumped down from the bar and ran for the kitchen as bullets smashed empty bottles, creating a shower of broken glass above her head.

Through the back door and out onto the street, Grasshead tripped and fell, scrambling back up again and straight into a wall of guards marching down. She turned back; the door leading back in was blocked similarly. She began running the other way down the street and was met yet again with a wall of Blue Guard preventing her escape.

The walls closed in, trapping her like the cell they'd kept her in originally, but she stuck to her guns, refusing to go down without a fight.

Bang!

One guard fell to the floor.

Bang!

Down went another.

She shot again, again, and again, putting bullets in guards in every direction, but they were relentless, filling the gaps in their formation as soon as they'd been made. Now, they created a circle around her, all aimed at her person, as she struggled to decide which one to take down next, rapidly switching between them.

'Somet… somet… somet… run but can't hide… whatever,' came a voice from behind her. She turned to face it. Lucky stumbled into the circle, swinging around an empty bottle in his left hand. He looked angry. 'Seems like you can't do neither.' With a yell of strength, he launched the bottle towards Grasshead. She ducked, and it pathetically collided with some shining blue armour and fell into the sand.

He flicked his head up. Grasshead knew he wanted her to drop the gun and raise her hands, but instead, she aimed directly between his eyes. Her middle finger caressed the thin strip of metal which held the life of the man she piercingly glared at. But he knew she was bluffing… she could tell from his smile; if she shot Lucky, then the guards would shoot her. Everything she'd done to survive would be for nothing, and there's no way she'd let that happen.

On the other hand, he'd only get paid if she was alive, and no amount of money was useful to a dead man. Not taking her eyes or her weapon off him, she reached forward with her bare foot and dug it hard into the sand, dragging it across in front of her so that she stood on one side and Lucky on the other. No sooner had she completed it did Lucky raise a foot and hover it over the boundary. He lowered it, raised the other, then repeated the action several times, teasing, crossing over again and again with a mischievous grin on his face. Then his expression changed, reverting to the anger he'd first entered the circle with.

'You know, you have *no* idea how much you's worth!' he screamed. 'You have no idea how much Honeywax and effort's gone into this manhunt!'

Of course, she had a pretty good idea in her own head about how much she was worth. It wasn't a high figure, not after the last few days. He might have known the value, but he didn't know the cost.

But if she was valuable to him, then he must be bluffing too. There was no way the Blue Guard would shoot first. He simply wouldn't risk it. If she was dead, then he wouldn't get paid. She'd heard his voice give the order to capture her alive. She smiled internally, realising she was, in fact, in complete control of the scenario. She was in charge.

Bang!

She shot the guard directly behind and to the left of Lucky, returning the gun to aim at him so as not to give him a chance to react.

'You're gonna come back with us to the City. We're gonna put you back in the cell and find you another seller. We're gonna attach a bracelet to your ankle, which will kill you if you try to escape.'

Bang!

The guard directly behind and to the right of him fell also.

'Your life belongs to me,' he whispered.

One bullet left. If she stopped to reload, they'd take the opportunity to capture her. She couldn't afford to give them that chance. There was only one way out, just one solution that might let her take back control, that might give her freedom.

She rotated the weapon towards herself and pointed it at the underside of her own chin. She wasn't entirely convinced that she was bluffing herself, but the hope was that it was enough to convince Lucky. *Am I bluffing?*

As the mischievous grin dropped, Grasshead saw the cogs in his thick little skull working. She worked it out along with him: If he stepped over the line, she killed herself, and he failed his mission. No Honeywax. No reward.

Alternatively, he could set her free and walk away. Let her live, or let her die. Either way, he'd lost. Right at the end, when nothing else mattered, would he chose life or death?

The smirk returned on Lucky's face as he raised his foot towards her. She closed her eyes...

To Eternity and Beyond

oc Holliday rowed back to the *Leisurely Ländler* twice that night.

On his first trip back, he took himself, Rocket, Veroushka, and a bound hunter. By their side, Kalma's armour lay disassembled at the base of the boat so that her true form, an almost impossibly tall body-builder-like figure, was revealed through a light-grey jumpsuit that covered her from neck to toe. He couldn't help but be impressed by, slightly in awe of, and completely frightened of her. With a scar on her rough but nuanced face, short spiky hair, even tied up, she had an indomitable presence. Rocket didn't seem at all affected by what had happened to her, merely quietly delighting in the judicial irony of Kalma now being the one tied up. Kalma herself had been quiet.

As soon as they'd climbed aboard, he'd asked Rocket to build a brig, a task to which she had agreed enthusiastically, grabbing her tools and heading straight for the crow's nest. Although technically Kalma had done nothing illegal, giving her free roam of the *Ländler* didn't sit right with him.

Spotting an array of cans lined up on the edge, Holliday had asked Rocket what they were for. Apparently, the wait for them to return from the island had been so intensely boring for Rocket, she'd resorted to breaking into Doc Holliday's room and borrowed one of his guns to practice her aim. Before she'd been kidnapped, that is. She'd gleefully demonstrated just how much she'd improved by lining up three empty cans on the edge of the ship and missing every single one of them.

Having arrived on the beach only minutes before Vale, Galileo and Leira, he now returned to the *Ländler* for the second time with his remaining friends, along with Kalma's remaining belongings. Leira, to his surprise, seemed rather more bubbly than usual, the excursion into a land so different to that of which she was used to clearly having done her some good. He'd didn't ask or even mention her change of behaviour, not wanting to ruin the moment for her.

They all exchanged stories of the island on their way back, Holliday's story about his near-death experience, in particular, seeming to prove Vale's theory about the island being alive, much to her delight.

Together, they came up with a theory: The island was alive, thanks to all the vitazate, and knew it was in danger from the hunter. When Holliday ate the mortazine berry ('For every chemical, there is an equal and opposite anti-chemical,' Galileo had speculated), the island had saved him and given him the visions as a warning, knowing that he and Veroushka could help.

Galileo handed over the vial of chemicals he'd collected, and Holliday stored it in his bandolier.

Climbing back onto the deck, he looked up to see Rocket putting the finishing touches on a small prison, balancing precariously twenty feet high, with Kalma already inside. With little concern for her own safety, she welded the base to the wood with a blowtorch that she wore like a harness. Kalma had both hands wrapped around the metal bars. He prayed Rocket had made them strong enough; it looked like the prisoner inside might be able to rip them out if she put half a mind to it, but he trusted the inventor to have considered that... at least, he thought he trusted her. Holliday dropped the hunter's armour on the deck.

'Don't think much of the portering! Can I get some room service up here?!' Kalma shouted down at him. He caught Leira giggling out of the corner of his eye and failed to keep a straight face himself.

'Careful!' the prisoner yelled at Rocket as a shower of sparks flew in her direction. 'You an inventor or demolitionist?'

'Ooh, got a mouth on this one, haven't we? Doc, what *have* we brought home?' replied Rocket in an equally snarky tone as she switched off her blowtorch and stepped up to face her opponent.

Holliday felt an insult match coming. He could do something about it... or...

'Yeah, it's about the size of your head. How short are you, six-foot?' retorted Kalma, her idea of small.

'Five ten. Five stars and ten out of ten.'

'You wish. You're an eight at best.'

There was an awkward silence as they both tried to figure out exactly what that meant. It didn't sound like much of an insult. Rocket clearly was expecting something she could clap back at but had nothing. Interesting. Rocket was speechless. That was new. Someone wolf-whistled—Vale at a guess. The two snapped out of their glaring contest.

'Anyway, cap'n, are all the repairs on the ship done?' he asked Rocket as she climbed down the rigging.

'Of course, what do you take me for?' she replied, jumping down the final few ropes. 'Although, if you find any of your rooms missing, I apologise in advance.'

'How can they find them if they're missing?' Kalma shouted down. Rocket merely rolled her eyes to Holliday and subtly made a gesture at him that'd have made even the most foul-mouthed of sailors blush a darker shade of red.

Rocket had summoned the crew for a team meeting. Leira didn't really want to be there. After the excitement of the previous day, she'd much rather have spent a good deal of time alone in her room. Alone or with Veroushka.

The group sat around the helm like an audience at the amphitheatre, and Kalma watched from above. Leira didn't think much of the hunter from the little she'd seen. She felt uncomfortable around her. Whenever she went near, her haunting eyes seemed to pierce her skin, like she was being singled out. It was a feeling Leira was used to, genetic differences having an effect on everyday life. She tried to hide her blue hair from the woman in the cage and tried not to let it remind her of how she'd been treated back in the City.

On stage, Rocket had something covered under a sheet. From what she could tell, it was short and thin, like the stump of a tree. With a spin and a flourish, Rocket unveiled... well... Leira didn't really know what it was. A quick glance at the others' faces confirmed that they had no idea either. The thing had a grill on the front, some buttons on the side, a black screen on the top and was attached to the floor with some kind of mast or pole. Three slow, sarcastic, and condescending claps echoed from the cell above.

'What is it?' queried Vale, parchment and quill in hand as always.

Rocket indicated towards it with a smug look on her face. Vale got up and walked over to it, tentatively reaching out to press...

'Not that button!' yelped Rocket, grabbing Vale's hand out of the way and guiding it towards the screen at the top.

'Czzz... Hello!' an omnipotent voice boomed. It sounded like Rocket, but Rocket hadn't spoken. One at a time, the non-incarcerated inhabitants joined Vale to watch what was happening.

'It's a... thing!' Rocket revealed proudly, her voice coming from her own mouth this time. 'Try asking it a question, Leira.'

Nervously, she approached the mast. She was on the spot; everyone was looking at her. All she had to do was come up with a good question. She was good at good questions, apparently. *You're on stage, Leira. Perform.* Why was her mind blanking now?!

'Er... err... why... do things... nicer... under water?' she spluttered out.

'I'm sorry, I do not understand. Please repeat the question with more competence to your sentence structure,' Rocket's machine replied. Leira turned away, shielding her reddened face.

'I call it the Ländler Entertainment, Information, and Relaxation Application!'

'You can't call it *Leira!*' Vale pointed out.

'How about... Virtual Artificial... no, that's not going to work either, is it?' mused Rocket, the entire crew simultaneously rolling their eyes. 'I've got it! Ship Entertainment Control Systems Interface!'

'No, you're not calling it—' Galileo interjected immediately before quietening down his tone, embarrassed at what he was about to say. 'Secsi...'

'Fine, I'll swap Control and Systems. Ship Entertainment Systems Control Interface: Sesci.'

The name seemed to suit everyone, apart from Kalma, who naturally proclaimed that it sucked.

'Excellent! Sesci it is,' concurred Rocket, tapping the new name of her machine on a typewriter at her control panel.

'Hello, I am... Sesci,' replied Sesci in Rocket's voice. Leira was sure this would never get confusing at all.

'She can record information, tell us information, but more importantly, she can play card games with us! And—!' Rocket continued with a flamboyant twirl, landing face to face with Leira and presenting her with something in her hands. Leira looked at it, a smile on her face as she realised that it was her butterfly-winged music player. She eagerly took it and clipped the earpiece onto herself, rotating the dial to select a song. She hit play on her favourite song.

The first moment she heard the melody was the best. It felt good to be able to hear it properly again, the singer in the recording being far more talented than she considered herself to be. But looking around, she realised that everyone seemed to be laughing. She unclipped the earpiece to see what was wrong. This was met with even more roars of laughter. She could still hear the music! It hadn't been coming from the earpiece at all; it was coming from Sesci's speaker grill! Leira quickly switched off the music and handed the device back to a red-faced Rocket, who offered to try again.

'Well, I hope that's not representative of your skills, else we might never set sail!' Kalma taunted. 'How does this old thing stay afloat anyhow?'

Rocket said nothing but walked back up to the helm and took hold of the wheel, hiding the grin on her face as she did so. Leira and the rest of the gang followed, each holding on tight to whatever they could find.

'Ready?!' Rocket shouted over her shoulder. Without waiting for an answer, she kicked over a lever to her right, tapped some keys on the typewriter to her left and spun the wheel clockwise as fast as she could. Leira felt the power surging underneath her. Up above, engines on a mast started rotating so frantically that Leira was sure they would take off on their own accord.

Slowly, the *Leisurely Ländler* started moving forwards, faster and faster, then finally it was up in the air. The wind blew at magnificent speeds through Leira's hair. Looking behind her, the island shrank with the distance, and the top of the waterfall that she'd spent the day in became a spec of blue in a sea of green and purple. It seemed to have stopped growing. In fact, she was sure it was actually shrinking. Why would it start shrinking as soon as they left? Had something *created* the island just for their safety? The same something who had guided her there, perhaps? Something... underwater? Galileo had theorised that the high levels of the vitazate chemical were a naturally occurring anomaly, but what if it wasn't? Something out there was following them, protecting them... her.

She looked up at the crow's nest to see Kalma's reaction and was not disappointed. She was desperately holding onto the bars, her jaw dropped all the way through the base of her cell, below the rigging and down into the hull.

'You okay up there?!' Rocket shouted, the captain having the time of her life. She got no response from the terrified bounty hunter.

159

Finally, the *Ländler* levelled out. Leira smiled. As Veroushka took her hand, she looked off into the horizon, wondering where they'd end up next. What magical science might they stumble across, and what glorious questions would she find out the answers to?

The Waters of Life

Two jungles,
Both alike in different ways,
Each has their hunters,
Each has their prey.

Roots send life to the top,
Hidden below where no one can see them,
Safe from gluttony and richer fare,
Freedom from freedom.

A built-in instinct,

The Two Jungles

For us all to survive,
A big, completed and sad word:
Alive.

- Galileo

128 Weeks Later

Something appeared on the horizon.

They'd been walking for days, but finally, they'd made it. She turned to her side; her hundred-strong army stood before the dried-up oasis, each of them equipped with a bag of seeds. The intense sunlight burnt her intensely wrinkled face.

By day, she'd spent the last two years scouting and recruiting the bandit towns in the desert, sneaking to and from the City, negotiating with the Gamin gangs and stealing everything she needed to start a civilisation.

By night, she'd researched. The elemental torch she'd picked up in the workshop contained a wealth of knowledge, and she'd been obsessed with unlocking it. The fire and the lightning buttons had been obvious enough, but the function of the third button—the infinity mesh—had been the biggest mystery.

She wasn't an artificer, but eventually, she'd worked it out. The final button contained some kind of life-chemical. It was the reason she'd grown so old so quickly. In small doses, it seemed to cure ailments and heal wounds. In larger doses, however, it aged, like it was speeding up life.

She lifted her frail arms and threw them forwards. Her tribe ran in front of her, planting their seeds in perfect curves around the sandy basin. She stood and watched with Robin the manta-rat perched on her shoulder, admiring their dedication and passion as they worked. She'd join in if she had the energy.

The sun descended, and it became nightfall. Her tribe had finished their work, and they returned to stand behind her. Her aide approached her.

'They're ready for you, Tawney,' said Zauré. The older woman smiled down at the younger one.

'Well then, We better get this party started, hadn't we?' she said. Tawney aimed her blowtorch at the ground, began winding and pressed the infinity mesh button one final time.

A bright glimmering light sparkled out of the end, homing in on the planted seeds. The light bounced around. The torch vibrated wildly in her hand, but she gritted her teeth and held it steady. Tree trunks sprouted in the immediate area, growing branches, leaves, and flowers.

Tawney released the button and stopped winding. The desert was plunged back into darkness. The silhouette of small newly formed trees was barely visible in front. Zauré handed her a soft-glass bag filled with shining light. Tawney unzipped it and reached inside, carefully pulling out a handful of luminons, making sure that she wasn't hurting them. She threw them into the trees, and the forest lit up, glowing vibrantly. Out here, where they were free, the luminons shone brighter than ever before.

It was spectacularly dense, beautifully green and full of life. She heard birds singing and insects buzzing. Tawney smiled and turned back to her tribe.

'Last one to the other side's a scrawny weasel!'

Screams of laughter and joy emanated from her tribe as she and Robin watched them sprint into the treeline.

Her work in the City wasn't complete. She'd worked out what they were doing there over the last two years. She knew the meaning of what she'd seen in the workshop, of the spider drones, and of the masts. She knew what it was leading to, and she vowed to return to stop it.

For now, though, she could relax.

She held out her arm, and Robin crawled down it, gliding to the ground and sprinting into the trees. Tawney laughed before walking in herself. The forest may not have been eternal, but creating her own eternity was a damn good start.

The Two Jungles

About the Author

Born and raised in Leeds, Delia currently works as a software developer. Apart from writing, she enjoys composing music and playing video games.

Her inspiration mostly comes from watching livestreams of cats on the internet. In fact, none of the stories are her own. The cats speak to her and tell her what to write. She feels it's her duty to tell their stories to the world. Her friends have told her that she should really seek help from a professional about this, but the only advice they could give was 'Meow, meow meow.'

Printed in Great Britain
by Amazon